THE
COOLABAH
CREEK
MAGGOT

PAUL FERRAR

For Pammy
with love

*This book was written on Ngunnawal land
and the author acknowledges its people as
the traditional owners of the land*

**To find out more about this book,
or to contact the author, please visit:
www.vividpublishing.com.au/paulferrar**

Copyright © 2022 Paul Ferrar

ISBN: 978-1-922788-35-1
Published by Vivid Publishing
A division of Fontaine Publishing Group
P.O. Box 948, Fremantle
Western Australia 6959
www.vividpublishing.com.au

A catalogue record for this
book is available from the
National Library of Australia

Rebel against the flesh and bone,
The word of the blood, the wily skin,
And the maggot no man can slay.

Dylan Thomas, Poem: Find Meat on Bones

KING: Now, Hamlet, where's Polonius?
HAMLET: At supper.
KING: At supper! Where?
HAMLET: Not where he eats, but where he is eaten:
a certain convocation of politic worms are e'en at him.
Your worm is your only emperor for diet: we fat all
creatures else to fatten us, and we fat ourselves for
maggots…

William Shakespeare, Hamlet, Act IV, Scene 1

GULF COUNTRY, NORTH WEST QUEENSLAND

L ike many corpses, Anna Ioannides was discovered by chance.

A lean and withered stockman was driving his mob of cattle to the edge of Coolabah Creek to drink, when he noticed them baulk at a patch of freshly turned earth and veer around it. As he drew level with it his nostrils picked up the stink of decaying meat.

'Them bastards 'ave 'ad another one o' me steers,' he muttered to himself. He'd lost a lot through stock thefts lately.

He dismounted from his horse and kicked with his boot at the earth. If the bastards had left the head he could at least tell by the clipped ear marks if it was his or not. His foot encountered something solid. He dug the point of his boot under it, and the toe came up with a human hand resting on it, as though clutching it for support.

He stared at it in disbelief, motionless for half a minute.

'Shit', he said.

Finally he bent down and covered it with earth again. He called off his two dogs which were now showing a bit of interest in the appealing smell.

'Git orn Tag, move 'em on. C'm'ere Gyp – keep 'em moving.' He remounted and rode back to his cattle, which were now strung out along the bank of the creek.

When the cattle had finished drinking he drove them across the shallow reach and on for several miles to his holding paddock, where they would stay until the stock transports came in a day or two to collect them for the meatworks. He made some running repairs to the fence near the gate, then remounted and rode slowly off towards the little township of Ironbark Creek.

He tethered his horse to the sign reading 'POLICE' and loped on bandy legs into the Police Station, which was the front room of the policeman's house. He rang the bell.

The policeman came in from the back. His uniform overalls were splattered with blood, because he mostly wore them when he was butchering an animal for the deep freeze, as now.

'G'day, Bill,' said the stockman.

'G'day, Norm.'

Jesus, just when I'm in the middle of doing a beast. I suppose the old bugger's noticed another one of his bullocks has gone.

'I found a body, Bill.'

Christ, just as I feared. The Stock Squad out from Cairns again, poking around and asking questions about all the meat in the freezer. I'll have to get Herb to do me some dockets again quick.

'Are you sure it was one of yours, Norm?'

'Not a steer, Bill, a person.'

Shit. That means I'll have to get the other carcase back out of the mortuary and into Herb's cold room, and I shan't be able to use the mortuary again till after the inquest. Wouldn't it give you the...

'Where was this, Norm?'

'Over at Coolabah Creek, Bill. You know where I takes me beasts across the water, over on the far bank there's a body. Someone's buried it under a heap o' dirt. Looked like a woman's hand I found.'

Gulp! Murder...

First instant scenario: brilliant solution of murder by local policeman, redeeming past indiscretions that led to original posting to Ironbark Creek; policeman commended by Commissioner. Second, more realistic scenario: Criminal Investigation Branch comes up from Brisbane to solve murder; local policeman has style cramped. But at least the CIB won't be worrying about unexplained meat around the place. Not that sort, anyway.

Sigh. 'You'd better take me out there, Norm...'

NICHOLAS TWISTLETON

I'm not a great fan of flying and I don't like it when it lurches around a lot, as our plane was at the moment. The only good thing was that the cabin display showed that we were now over central Queensland, and heading directly for our destination, Sydney. The cabin crew had served enormous numbers of breakfasts and were now trying to clear them away, in competition with streams of passengers heading to the toilets for a last wash and brush-up before landing. About half the breakfasts seemed to have been eaten; the remainder had been left by passengers zombified after over twenty hours of flying from London. We'd at least broken our journey in Bangkok for a couple of days.

My companion, Marion MacTaggart, doesn't share my view of flying – she loves it. She'd eaten every scrap of her breakfast, and then taken over mine and polished that off too. She doesn't reject food except in the direst of circumstances.

We'd met while working for doctorates in East Africa, doing research on birds. Without either of us saying anything our lives had gradually entwined, and most people nowadays take us for a married couple. We both work at a university in England, Marion as a research fellow and me as a lecturer, but we're about to spend six months sabbatical leave in Australia.

Somehow the breakfasts did get cleared away in time, and more remarkably the passengers were all back in their seats as the plane descended over Sydney. Marion was beside a window and was making *ooh* and *aah* noises as we descended over the harbour. I had a good view of the aircraft wing, which I was pleased to see was still attached to the plane.

The plane banked and turned for its final approach, and then with a big bump we were down. In the terminal we collected our bags, and underwent a thorough Customs examination because we were carrying quite a lot of equipment for fieldwork with us. Finally we went out into the reception area, and Marion went quickly forward to greet a tall, slender, immaculately dressed woman – her sister Moira. I'd met Moira once before in England, and I still find it hard to believe that they're sisters – there can't be many common genes between them. Where Moira is tall and slim, Marion could be described as short and dumpy, though never to her face. In temperament she's like her father, an Edinburgh physician now retired to Inverness for the climate and the fly-fishing. Like him she has energy, enthusiasm and a short way with the fools of the world. Moira, like her mother, attracts words such as style, poise, coolness and elegance. She's the founder and co-owner of Flaire, a respected and very profitable design consultancy in a chic part of old Sydney.

To my great relief the greetings seemed genuinely warm – one possible hurdle over. On previous occasions in Britain there had been some spectacular family feuding. Moira considered her little sister an uncouth tomboy, who'd not only failed to find a ladylike occupation in life, but had positively opted for something as disgusting as biology. All that cutting up of animals. Marion for her part had described Moira (within her hearing) as prim, stuck-up and suffering from severe anal retention. Moira had made references to Marion living in sin with a person of equally low morals, not really an appropriate description of me. Marion had retorted that Moira was a professional virgin, an unkind comment since Moira is married. However, time and twenty thousand kilometres separation appear to have done their proverbial thing, and peace seems in prospect at least for a while.

A man who'd been standing slightly back while the reunion took place then stepped forward and was introduced as Fergus O'Riordan, Moira's husband. He was an amiable-looking, slightly bear-like man, and he seemed to be quite gentle. I know that he's a biochemist who leads a research team at Sydney University. They're investigating a new substance as a possible cure for cancer, and their work has achieved world renown. Moira must be able to tolerate messy subjects when they're as prestigious as that. Both partners work very hard, and they've never had children.

Greetings completed all round, we went out to the car park and up to a gleaming BMW – deep blue in colour, and evidently not one of the cheapest in the range. Moira drove with Marion beside her. Fergus and I, who are both long in the leg, squeezed into the back, though it was less cramped than the backs of some cars I've been in.

The airport environs were disappointing – rather like the

industrial parts of almost any city – but they improved as we neared the city centre. We passed through an area that seemed to have a lot of strip clubs, and then we were on a road that ran along Sydney Harbour. At last the views were what I'd hoped for. The houses became more opulent, and the gardens lusher and larger. Finally we reached what Moira announced as Vaucluse, where she and Fergus lived.

The car swung down a steep, shrub-lined driveway, curved so that one could only see the roof of the house from the road. At the bottom Moira paused to press a button on a small gadget tucked into the parcel tray, and one of the two garage doors at the side of the house rolled up for them to enter.

Marion had told me that it would probably be a nice house since Moira and Fergus were well off (filthy rich was how she put it), but I wasn't prepared for the reality. The house was half open-plan, generously proportioned in all rooms, and furnished throughout in simple but exquisite taste. But it wasn't a sterile display of design but a house one could live in, and comfortably. Small wonder that Moira was such a successful designer. The construction was split-level, to follow the slope of the hill and to take fullest advantage of the stunning view of Sydney Harbour. You couldn't fault it.

Deckchairs were set out in the small, pleasantly-landscaped garden that sloped down from the house, and we sat there sipping coffee. We also drank in the remarkable view of Sydney Harbour, right across to the Harbour Bridge and the Opera House. Assorted birds flew in and out of the garden, some of which I could identify and others not. Brilliantly coloured parrots were the most spectacular – a delight for an ornithologist. We chatted for a while, relaxing as the stress of long air travel fell away, and then accepted the suggestion of a little nap. Which turned into hours of unbroken sleep for both of us, as Moira had known it would, so she'd had no reservations in accepting an invitation to speak at a charity dinner for artists' widows and children at a Sydney hotel that evening.

* * *

After a couple of gentle days chez O'Riordan, Marion and I were both feeling that we should stop being idle and justify our trip to Australia. Marion had arranged to undertake a study in outback Queensland of the mortality caused to new-born lambs by birds of prey and carrion crows, in return for which she'd been given a modest grant and the use of a government vehicle in Queensland. My specialised field, the study of tits, wasn't possible over here because Australia didn't have any tits. Not the avian sort, anyway. But I was lucky enough to persuade a conservation organisation to give me a small amount of money to study the significance of waterholes in the ecology of birds of arid Australia. Not much, but it'll be better than nothing.

Fergus O'Riordan had made some useful contacts for us to help arrange the projects, and he was giving us an account of this one evening over glasses of a rather nice Australian botrytised wine when the telephone rang. Moira went to answer it, but then came back to say it was for Fergus.

When Fergus re-entered the room his face was drained of colour. He looked at Moira and said: 'Anna's been murdered. Her body was found near a creek in the back of beyond in Queensland.'

He dropped heavily into his chair, and his hand was shaking

as he picked up his glass of wine and drained it. He sat looking stunned.

There was silence for a moment, then Moira said, with rather pursed lips: 'Well, I can't say I'm entirely surprised. I always told you something like that would happen to her.' She must then have realised that that sounded harsh because she added: 'I'm sorry to hear it, though. Do they know who did it?'

'Max didn't say.' Fergus turned to us. 'Anna was an assistant of mine in the unit until a few months ago. It's come as a terrible shock.'

He got up to replenish our glasses, and when he sat down again he attempted to revive the previous conversation about our projects. But his mind clearly wasn't on it, and the talk drifted on to other topics.

As I lay in bed that night I couldn't help thinking about this awful event. Although it must come as a shock to anyone to be told that someone you know has been murdered, I instinctively felt that Fergus's reaction was different from mere shock. Perhaps there'd been a bit of a feeling of bereavement as well? Was she someone with whom Fergus had been having an affair? That would account for Moira's rather callous attitude. When Moira had shown us round the house I'd noticed that she and Fergus slept in separate rooms, and I'd sensed that their relationship was that of good friends rather than ardent bedmates. Could Fergus, only in his forties and not unattractive, really be leading an entirely sexless life? Surely one can't become so dedicated to research that any other emotional outlet becomes unnecessary?

But I must have fallen asleep before I came to any conclusion.

* * *

The next day Moira and Marion went into Sydney to meet some cousin or other of the family, and Fergus invited me to accompany him to the university. It was ostensibly to make further arrangements for our work in Queensland, but I thought that he seemed rather keen to have some company that morning. Perhaps he didn't want to be alone after his disturbing news of the previous evening. Or maybe he just wanted to show his beloved project to someone.

We drove to the campus of the University of Sydney, a pleasant oasis in a rather dingy area, possessed of the same parking problems as most university campuses throughout the world. Fergus fortunately had a reserved parking space; even more fortunately nobody else was in it.

His building was unprepossessing from the outside, but very much the reverse inside. A marble-floored hallway, white-coated figures scurrying down pleasantly panelled corridors, a fresh, slightly hospital smell about it all. Smiles from a middle-aged receptionist sitting at a switchboard almost lost among pot-plants. Her cheery 'Morning, Fergus!' suggested he was well-liked by staff.

We walked down one of the corridors, and through open doorways I could see laboratories filled with intricate arrangements of glass equipment, huge microscopes that must each have cost his salary for several years, radioactivity signs everywhere, electron microscope rooms... It all looked like real science, compared to my own string and sealing wax stuff. I don't usually need more than binoculars, a field notebook and a table to dissect the occasional bird on, and I felt a bit intimidated by this ultra-professional atmosphere.

Fergus's office, however, was more relaxing, and the easy chair beside a coffee table was most comfortable. Fergus dropped into one beside me and began to stare into space. After several minutes of silence, I murmured:

'Are you thinking of your assistant who died?'

Fergus started slightly as though he hadn't realised I was still there.

'Yes.' He continued to stare into space.

'Were you emotionally involved with her?' I asked gently. Somehow Fergus was the sort of person you could put a question like that to.

'Yes,' he said bleakly. 'Rather a lot, actually. But you'll get entirely the wrong impression from that. We weren't lovers – it was a father and daughter relationship if it was anything.'

He turned to face me.

'Perhaps it would do me good to talk about her – it might exorcise the memory a little. The problem is to know what words to use – she was a hard enough person to understand, let alone explain.

'Her father's Greek, as you might guess from her surname – Ioannides. He's the owner of a huge meat-processing plant in Melbourne. He cans meat and pet-food, makes hamburger patties, salamis, frankfurts, delicatessen – just about anything that involves the processing of meat. I met him once and he wasn't a person who appealed to me, though I'd have to admit he's a good businessman. He's a hard, aggressive man of set ways and ideas. He has the reputation of being a bastard to

11

work for – the Sunday papers are always doing exposés and unflattering articles. Most of his employees are migrants because most other Australians wouldn't put up with the wages and conditions that he offers. The migrants are usually desperate for work, or lacking work permits or something, so they'll accept anything.

'One of his set views is that women don't work, except in the house where they wait hand and foot on their adored lord and master. His wife is just like that, a complete mousy nonentity, but unfortunately for him his daughter wasn't, and she inherited his temperament and stubbornness. She had flaming rows, was locked in the house, even worse I suspect, until she was twenty-one. After that he couldn't hold her, though she nearly had to go to court to establish the fact.

'She got a bottle-washing job here and started doing a laboratory assistant's course at the Tech, and she did brilliantly at it. She had a first-class brain. If she hadn't had the trouble at home she could have had an outstanding university career and would probably have been on this project as a postdoctoral research worker. It was an appalling waste – **why** did it have to happen...?'

He paused for a long moment, and then went on.

'Anyway, when she got her diploma we upped her to a technical grade, and she became my personal assistant. She picked up the scientific side amazingly fast. She was good at the practical work, but more remarkably she was able to make constructive suggestions about the development of the research. It was like having a very pleasant and stimulating colleague.'

He turned to face Nicholas again.

'It's odd how some people just hit it off together. It can

happen between two men, that they derive great contentment from each other's company, and it occurs between women as well. It **can** also happen between a man and a woman, but I suspect less often because sexual complications usually arise. But the feeling I'm talking about isn't overtly sexual and I think not even covertly. It's more a social thing, the satisfying of a need to feel a communal being. It was like that between Anna and myself.'

He turned away and lapsed into silence again. I said nothing, confident that more would surface in time.

'If that had been all it would have been marvellous,' continued Fergus, with a note of bitterness in his voice, 'but you can't have a background like Anna's without being screwed up somewhere. The manifestation of hers was that she threw herself at almost any male who was around. She would practically seduce them, whether they were initially interested or not, and then she'd suddenly round on them, shriek at them, abuse them and reject them. We had one or two very embarrassing incidents with visiting scientists. The whole trouble was that what she wanted, and desperately needed, was love and affection, but all she ever got of course was sex. She had a completely dotty conception of what men were like. After most of these occurrences she'd come and cry on my shoulder, sometimes literally. That's what I meant when I said ours was a father and daughter relationship. I loved her, but it was the affection of a sympathetically inclined human being for another who's in trouble and needs help. And Anna trusted me completely as a recipient for tears and confidences, and as an adviser.' He gave me a sad little smile. 'You've no idea what a rewarding experience that is.

'Anyway, even that couldn't go on forever. Anna was here for six years in all, but finally she told me that she had to leave for a while to find herself. It broke my heart, but I always believed that she might eventually come back here to work. And now she won't...

'She handed in her notice about three months ago and went up north. I had one postcard from her.' He handed me a card that had been propped on the corner of his desk. 'You can read it.'

The card showed a golden beach surrounded by granite boulders and coconut palms, and an inscription that read "Greetings from Magnetic Island". It was postmarked Townsville, and in a neat, firm hand was written:

Dear Ferg,
Made it this far. Coincidence - I've met a guy whose family ships cattle regularly to my dad in Melbourne. I've got a job as a chambermaid in a hotel. You wouldn't believe how yukky some people leave their rooms. Haven't found my salvation yet. Perhaps I never will.

Love Anna.

There were two chaste little kisses beside the signature.

I gave the card back to Fergus.

'Was Anna an attractive girl?'

'It depends on how you define attractive. She was a bit skinny and angular, and she had a long face with a prominent Greek nose. But she wasn't ugly. She moved with athletic litheness, and there was what you might call an animal sexuality about her.'

'And you still say you weren't sexually attracted to her?' I asked, very gently.

Fergus stared at the carpet with a rueful expression.

'No, I suppose I can't honestly say that,' he replied slowly. 'I still get the odd twinges when I look at any young maidens, but whenever I've tried to do anything about it in the past it hasn't been a great success, so I've given up trying. It's easier that way. The good thing about Anna was that she never seemed to expect me to do anything of that sort, and I could relax completely with her. Funny, that, when she chased almost every other man around here. I suppose I should have felt insulted, but I didn't. I resigned myself to that situation.' He continued to stare at the carpet.

'I'm very sorry,' I said. 'It's a most unhappy business.' The words were entirely inadequate, but I couldn't think of anything useful to say and Fergus remained plunged in gloom.

Suddenly he gave a little snort and said:

'I've just remembered. I've actually got Anna on tape, though she never knew it. It's one of her typical ends of affairs. It's not a very good recording, but would you like to hear it?'

'Mm', I said as non-commitedly as I could. It seemed quite gruesome to think of listening to the voice of someone who was now violently dead, especially in such a situation, but Fergus seemed keen. I wondered how on earth Fergus could have such a thing on tape.

'I should explain how I came to have it,' said Fergus. He must have seen my look of surprise. 'We get lots of leading cancer scientists here, many from overseas. We always ask them to give a seminar on their work, and we always tape the seminars so we don't miss any interesting information. Not that anyone gives away much in a cut-throat field like this. However, we try.

'We'd been having trouble with our old microphone, which used to pick up audience noise better than it did the voices of the people who were speaking, so we decided to buy a new directional microphone. The day it arrived I'd rigged it up in my lab and was wondering how to test it when Anna started a row in the adjoining room. The connecting door was half open, and I couldn't resist trying it. I felt terrible afterwards, and thank God Anna never found out or it would have been the end of even our beautiful friendship. She was ditching a vacation student we'd had working temporarily in the lab. He was a nice lad – I felt quite sorry for him. They were moving around a bit as they spoke, and it was the perfect chance to see how well I could track voices. I didn't do it very well as you'll hear from the fades, because I couldn't let Anna see I was doing it so I didn't know quite where to point it, but I did get a certain amount of it. I should have scrubbed the tape straight afterwards; I don't know why I didn't but I didn't.'

He took a cassette player from a corner cupboard, then rummaged at the back of a desk drawer until he found a cassette. He put it in, wound it back, and set it to "Play".

The tape started with switch noises, then clicks and interference from the microphone being jolted, and then a rather intermittent conversation could be heard. Anna's voice was rich and surprisingly deep for a woman, but the first voice was a man's.

'......dinner somewhere and then go to a show or something.'

'What the hell would I want to go............you for?'

'......did the other night. I enjoyed it – I thought you did too?'

'......sure you did. Free rooting............the night! It's all right for you............ got raped.'

'Christ Almighty............talking about? You were practically begging me to do it!'

'......pity you couldn't do it then isn't it? ....limp shrimp you call a prick. You'd better learn what to do with it if you want a real............'

'Jesus, there was nothing wrong............frigid bitch!'

'Frigid, shit I'm not frigid! You just don't............play with the typists, little boy. I'll find a MAN when I want......'

This was followed by a crash of breaking glass, a click, and then the tape was silent. Fergus turned it off.

'Not very edifying, is it? I shouldn't have played it to you because it'll give you completely the wrong impression of Anna. She wasn't like that at all. She just got a kind of madness when she tried to relate to men. Come on, let's go to the lab and get some coffee. My new assistant always keeps a pot on the boil. I couldn't face the main tea room at the moment. The news'll be out and they'll all be talking about Anna.'

* * *

I must say that I found the events around Anna quite disturbing, and again I was lying in bed thinking about the whole sad mess. Two people, each with personal problems, had found comfort and solace in each other, and now it was all destroyed. Fergus would recover – not completely, because I don't think anyone's ever quite the same after an experience like that – but for Anna there'd be no recovery. Someone had denied her any chance of that.

How had it happened? Was it quite casual, or did some horrible episode like that tape lead up to it? Or was there quite a different reason? One person presumably still knew, but the chances that he or she would ever be revealed were probably pretty slight. If a body's found somewhere as remote as the outback, how does one even go about looking for clues? You can hardly question all the witnesses. As Fergus had said, what a waste, what a crying, terrible waste...

NICHOLAS

It was time to leave. Sabbaticals don't last forever, and too much of this one had already gone. Marion had air-freighted a box of equipment to Queensland, and we took our leave of Moira and Fergus and flew to Brisbane where we were to collect Marion's government car. This turned out to be a four-wheel drive Toyota station wagon, comfortable, roomy and well suited to the varied requirements of our field projects.

We collected the box of equipment, and decided to leave Brisbane while it was still light. We made an involuntary tour of several suburbs while we searched for the correct main road, and finally found the Bruce Highway running north. The trip provided me with my first surprise. I'd always imagined that the north of Australia would be covered by jungle, at least in the more coastal parts. However, we found ourselves driving through a mixture of eucalyptus forest, pine plantations, sugarcane, pineapples, and a thick swamp forest of what I recognised as melaleuca and leptospermum. Then the country became drier and we were amongst cattle; brown shorthorns, some crossed with Herefords, some with more exotic breeds. Every now and then a sign would advertise a Brahman stud and we'd see fields of bulls, white and humped like Indian sacred cattle, moving ponderously along like mobile tents, their long, corrugated dewlaps waving like loose flysheets and their pizzles hanging like tent poles gone awry.

We reached Maryborough for the first night and Mackay for the second. From there we followed the coastal highway as far as Giru, then took a back road that cut a corner to the main road leading inland to Mount Isa and ultimately to Darwin. I had a bit of a pang when I realised that by doing that we were bypassing Townsville, only a few miles further up the road and the last place from which Anna Ioannides had made human contact, at least with Fergus. But it would have been pointless to go through there specially for that, and anyway Fergus had said that her body was found somewhere in the Queensland outback.

We followed the Mount Isa road as far as Charters Towers, and then struck off north-west along a fine bitumen road laid for a new nickel smelter at Greenvale. After the smelter the road deteriorated greatly, and we opted out at Georgetown where we spent the night in an old wooden hotel. It had evidently once been stylish, but was now seriously crumbling.

Next day, after an unmemorable breakfast we set out along another bad, corrugated gravel road into ever drier country – burnt brown grass, stunted trees and shrubs, parched soil that threw up dust at the slightest excuse, and a shimmering heat haze over everything. We stopped at Gilbert River to ask the way to our destination. The garage attendant gave us a rather sceptical look and directed us north along a narrow dirt track whose sign said "Dunbar 223". It wasn't clear whether the 223 was miles or kilometres – probably miles from the age of the sign – but it didn't really matter because we weren't going as far as Dunbar Station. The Queensland Institute of Entomological Research had established a small field laboratory in the north-east corner of Miranda Downs, and it was there that our contacts for advice and assistance were at present working.

We nearly missed the little sign at the side turning that read Q.I.E.R., but there was a larger name-plate at the entrance to the camp. Beneath it someone had tacked to the pole "Welcome to Flyblown Downs", which was somehow appropriate to the feel of the place. Two long caravans and a small one stood under open shelters roofed with corrugated iron, and two medium sized tents had been erected near a tree. A water tank stood on a tower of wooden poles, fed by what looked like a small pump at the base of one of the supports; the lower part of the tower was screened with sacking. A telephone line ran to one of the caravans from a nearby tree, and a slatted wooden shed that looked like a toilet had been placed at a discreet distance from everything.

And that was all.

Hm...

* * *

Marion pulled the station wagon to a halt in the dusty centre of the camp, and a figure appeared at the door of one of the caravans – a young man in shorts, khaki shirt and leather boots.

'Hi! You wouldn't be Marion and Nicholas by any chance?'

'We would,' replied Marion. 'Good morning. I think it's still morning.'

'Gil said you'd probably get lost being Poms,' said the young man coming over, 'but I told him not everyone's as stupid as he is. I'm Mike Tandouris.'

'How do you do,' said Marion. 'Are you Gil's assistant?'

'No, I work for Frank Feeney. He's out in the bush at the moment, and so's Gil. They sometimes leave me back here to do the important work.' He made all his comments with a cheerful insouciance that robbed them of offensiveness. 'They said if you showed up for me to bed you down. Not literally, of course,' he added, looking at Marion.

'We don't have enough tents for you to have a private one, but we've screened off half of this one. Frank sleeps in the other end – as far as anyone knows he doesn't snore. Gil and I share half the other one, and the rest of it's our store room. The two big trailers are laboratories, and the caravan's basically a kitchen cum workshop. The dunny's over there – you can see the vent pipe above the bushes. And that's about it.'

'How do you wash yourselves?' asked Marion, who was probably feeling as dusty as I was. 'Just at a bowl?'

'Oh no, we've got a shower – I forgot that. Come and see,' he added – he must have seen my look of surprise.

He led us to the water tower, and inside the screening we saw a shower nozzle fastened to one of the legs, with a pipe leading down from the water tank. Half a tin had been fastened below it for a soap dish.

'Cold, of course,' said Mike, 'but it's much better than a bucket, and it does actually warm up a bit when the sun's been on the tank all day. The pump comes on automatically when the level drops, so you don't have to worry about running out. It's all a bit simple, I'm afraid, but you get used to it.'

'Very similar to what we had for a couple of years when we worked in African game parks,' said Marion. 'Brings back happy memories!'

Mike helped us unload our car, then left us to unpack and get organised. After we'd finished and had a wash we found lunch already prepared for us, and life began to seem more civilised than had first appeared possible.

When we'd eaten, Mike said:

'Gil suggested you might like to go out and meet him if you turned up in time. I can tell you where to find him.' He hesitated. 'Do you...er...know what he's doing out there?'

We both shook our heads.

'Best I don't enlighten you then. You'll find out soon enough. Go back to the road from Gilbert River to Dunbar that you came along, and turn left towards Dunbar. You'll see his station wagon parked about three kilometres further on. Let's just say he'll have company, but you'll be able to tell which one's Gil.'

With some mystification we followed the instructions, and found Gil's vehicle with no trouble. It was parked near the carcase of a cow that presented a grotesque spectacle. It had swollen up in the tropical heat so that its belly was a taut, distended barrel, from which the four legs splayed outwards at exaggerated angles. The lips had shrivelled back to expose a grinning set of teeth, through which protruded a swollen, curling tongue. The whole thing was like an obscene inflatable toy, and it stank.

A figure crouched by the balloon's anal orifice, alternately peering through a hand-lens at the hide and pulling bits off with forceps and dropping them into a small glass vial. The figure waved.

'G'day! You must be Marion and Nicholas. I'll be with you in a moment.'

We stood back at a respectable distance, where the smell was less sickening and the hum of blowflies less obtrusive, and waited until the figure came to join us.

'How do you do? I don't think you'll want to shake hands at the moment, but I'm Gil Reynolds. Good trip up?'

'Not too bad,' I replied. 'We're beginning to acquire the taste of the local dust quite well now.'

'Yeah, it's not bad up here. You've no idea how much it improves the beer that you have after it.'

Gilbert Reynolds was a tall, lean, slightly stooping man, with an amiable face much tanned and wrinkled by the sun. He was every Englishman's idea of the typical Australian bushman, and not at all how I'd conceived an Australian research scientist. But Fergus had told us that he and Gil had been contemporaries as university students, and he had great respect for Gil's abilities.

Gil spoke with a soft but pronounced Australian accent, and delivered everything in a dry voice suggesting deep and permanent cynicism. We discovered in time that he was indeed cynical, but only to a moderate degree and with a pleasant humanity beneath it. It was perhaps a reaction to the arduous conditions under which he lived and worked.

'What are you doing?' asked Marion. 'Collecting flies?'

'In a manner of speaking, yes,' replied Gil. 'I'm actually sampling the larvae that'll later turn into flies – not that they have much hope after I've pickled them in this stuff.' He held up his vial, which was full of plump white maggots lying in a clear fluid. 'It's one way to make a living, I guess. Has Mike settled you in yet?'

'Yes, very well. He's been the model of hospitality.'

'Yeah, he's not a bad lad. But don't tell him I said so. I've made a few of the enquiries you mentioned in your letter, but this isn't the best place to tell you about them. I'd best finish my sampling, and then we can discuss things back at the camp over a beer. I'll be about another hour here. If you want to use the time to advantage you could go on up the track that way...' – he pointed past the cow – '...until you get to the first junction left. It's about five or six kilometres, but you can't miss it – there's a striking white ghost gum standing at the corner.'

He picked up a stick, and squatting in the dust began to draw a plan.

'Now when you turn left you go along until you come to a V-junction. Take the left fork, go past where the track does a wiggle like this, and just at the next straight bit you'll see wheelmarks going right. They lead through to a billabong that might do quite well for Nicholas. If you approach it quietly you might see some waterfowl on it. You can't miss it.'

'Positive about that?' I murmured, grinning faintly. I'd had those sorts of bush directions before, in Africa.

'Sure, it's easy. If you get to the sea you've gone too far – a long way too far. If you aren't back by six we'll come looking. Good hunting!'

And he went back to his carcase.

We found the billabong in the end, though it wasn't anything like as easy as Gil had made out. He'd probably known that too – perhaps he was checking on how well we'd manage. We came upon the lagoon suddenly and too abruptly, and a pair of waterfowl flew off as we stopped, but other birds were flying in and out of the trees and it was a pleasant place at which to rest.

I looked around, and decided it would make a congenial spot for my study.

When we returned to the camp we saw Gil's collecting clothes hanging from a tree well away from the tents, and Gil himself emerging from the shower. Two vehicles were parked in the corner of the clearing. As well as Gil's station wagon there was a Mini-Moke with an odd contraption on its roof, like a folding soft-top made of gauze. Its owner, a short, tubby, middle-aged man with a trim moustache, came out of the tent as we pulled to a halt, and was introduced as Frank Feeney. Mike was busy stoking a fire under a metal grid, and rather to my surprise I saw a pile of skewered kebabs lying on a tray beside it.

Five minutes later chairs had been set around the fire, and we all sat down to drink beer. There was a companionable silence, broken only by the crackling of the fire competing with the noise of slurped beer.

'It's a hard life in the bush, isn't it?' observed Gil with a faint grin. 'Just think of all those poor bastards at the Institute going home through the Brisbane rush-hour at the moment. I had two cars pass me all day. One was the mail service to Dunbar and Koolatah, and the other was a couple o' Poms looking for some waterhole or other. I sent them off on a wild goose chase through the bush – don't suppose they ever found it...' He was peering at us with quizzical amusement.

'We found it,' I said. 'And the wild goose, only it flew off just as we arrived.'

'You'll never believe what we saw along the way, though,' said Marion. 'There was this strange man bent double over a rotten cow pulling bits off it. It certainly is a weird country this!'

'Well I never,' said Gil. 'Musta been one of those government assistance fellers. The government pays people to do all sorts of crazy things these days to keep the unemployment figures down.'

'As a matter of interest, why exactly are you doing it?' I had to ask.

'For the money,' muttered Frank.

'True, old son,' replied Gil. 'It does come in handy at times. But what the gentleman means is why should the government pay me money to do it? I'm making a survey of all the different fly larvae of northern Australia.'

'He's going to write a book on them,' said Frank. 'It'll be called "All you ever wanted to know about maggots but were too disgusted to ask".'

'Is this mainly for academic interest?'

'Well, partly. There's quite a push in Australia at the moment to survey the flora and fauna, just to find out what's here. But this one's mainly for practical reasons. Maggots turn up as pests in quite a few situations, and we need to be able to identify them immediately without having to wait to rear them to adult flies. At the moment there's no good key to identification. There's also some quarantine nasties like screw-worm on Australia's doorstep in Papua New Guinea and Irian Jaya. We have to keep a close watch for them getting in here, with all our cattle. And then of course there's one field in which this becomes very important, which is forensic entomology.'

'Stiffs,' observed Mike.

Marion shuddered. 'You mean you have to bend over bodies like you were today and pull maggots out?'

'No, the police forensic people do all that. But I'm now

classed as an expert witness on the subject, so they send them to me for identification afterwards. I have to name the species, specify the stage of development, then check local temperatures and other weather factors, and then from all those data estimate the possible time of death. After that the hardest bit of all is convincing counsel for the defence that you actually know what you're talking about!'

'And do you?' I asked.

Gil leaned back with his hands behind his head. 'Of course, m'lud.' He grinned. 'But I do believe it. People like me have been studying blowflies for years – the usual fascination for the bizarre and macabre. But they found that the different species come to corpses in a pretty exact sequence, and each has its set time for development which is exactly correlated with temperature. The thing you've got to be careful about is the position of the body – if it's in deep shade or something the temperatures may be harder to work out. And of course if it's buried there'll be few flies or none at all, unless it was exposed at the surface for a little while first. There's usually more beetles than anything when the bodies are underground, but they're harder to set times with.'

'So if all that's known already, why are you doing the studies up here?' asked Marion.

'Well, it's mainly for quarantine, this trip. We don't really know all that much about blowflies in northern Australia, apart from the common ones with wide distributions, and I mentioned the screwworm in Papua New Guinea. It doesn't wait for its meal to become dead meat – it attacks live cattle and creates horrible lesions. We don't have it in Australia yet, but it'd do a lot of harm to our cattle industry if it got in. It's only just across the water, and we want to be able to spot it the moment it gets in here, but that means being able to recognise all the native species as well.'

'You wouldn't think we'd be prepared to sit down to dinner with someone like that, would you,' said Frank. 'Even worse, at times he gets forensic ones from corpses sent up by the police.'

'Well, as it happens I've got a couple of collections at the moment, to work on in my spare time when I get a bit. Matter of fact, one of them was from quite near here. Some girl that was found near Ironbark Creek, which is about fifty k's north of here. They got a great bottleful out of her – she must have been really humming.'

I suddenly felt an uncomfortable sensation, which gripped my middle and spread slowly outwards. 'That wasn't a girl called Anna Ioannides, was it?' I asked, trying to sound non-chalant but not succeeding.

'I don't know, they don't give me the names. But I've noticed in the past that the code number of the samples seems to contain the victim's initials, if they know who it was. I'll go and have a look if you like.'

He went into one of the large caravans and came back to say:

'Well, that particular sample's got "MAI" in its reference, so I guess it's possible. Friend of yours?'

'Friend of a friend. She was a research assistant in Sydney with Marion's brother-in-law, in fact you know him – Fergus? She was recently found murdered, but all he told us was "in outback Queensland".'

'Well, you can't get much outer-back than Ironbark Creek. There's various places in this country that lay claim to the title of the arsehole of Australia, but Ironbark Creek's the authentic one. In my opinion, anyway. God help the girl if she finished up there. I can't imagine a sadder end.'

There was silence for a moment, and Mike leaned over and put the kebabs on the fire. Tangy smells of barbecuing wafted around their seats, but I found I was no longer hungry. As the meat curled up and little drips of fat fell into the fire, all I could think of was Anna's body, full of maggots. The voice I'd heard on the tape; the person who still lived, if only in Fergus's memory. I hoped that Fergus would never hear about Anna's legacy to forensic science. If indeed it had been Anna.

The kebabs sputtered and sizzled, and when they were cooked Mike pulled some baked potatoes from the edge of the fire. The others were evidently less squeamish than me, because they pulled the meat from the skewers and tucked in with gusto.

'I'm glad you made it today,' said Gil. 'We'd been keeping the last capsicums for this dish, and I don't think they'd have survived another day. Frank brought them from Cairns last week – green vegetables are very hard to get out here.'

The thought that the peppers had also been almost decayed was suddenly too much for me. I pushed my plate aside and pleaded an upset stomach. My embarrassment at having to leave their prized meal was alleviated by Marion, who true to form managed to polish off everything that I'd left.

After the dinner had been cleared up I was able to cope with some coffee, and we sat in the open enjoying the peace and beauty of the outback evening. Occasional bats flew past our heads, dark and so fast that they were only half perceptible. Crickets began to chirp, and biting insects made their attentions known.

'I thought you were supposed to have caught all these bloody midges with that trap thing of yours,' Gil said to Frank, swatting at his ankles.

'Oh no, we only take a sample. Can't upset the balance of nature,' replied Frank. 'Anyway they're not attacking me.'

'That's because of that revolting oil you rubbed on your legs earlier. It'll give you skin cancer, that stuff. Anyway, I'm going inside the van. Anyone for a game of cards?'

Frank turned to Marion. 'I don't suppose you play bridge, do you?'

Marion gave me a hesitant glance. 'Well, yes, we do actually. We're not very good, though.'

'Ahhhh,' said Frank.

'Ahhhh,' said Gil.

'Bewdy!' said Frank.

'Ripper!' said Gil.

'Oh Christ,' said Mike. 'I'm going to see Miranda.'

'Welcome to membership of the Flyblown Downs Bridge Club,' said Gil. 'Social bridge a speciality, only we've been in recess for a while owing to lack of enrolment. Thanks to a hundred per cent increase in membership we're back in business.' He turned to Frank. 'Get out the eyeshades, old son.'

'Who's Miranda?' asked Marion.

'Her name's Lorraine, actually. She's a jillaroo over at Miranda Downs.'

'A whateroo?'

'Jillaroo. From jackaroo, which is a young guy working on a cattle or sheep station to get some experience, only she's better looking. She's a nice lass, actually.' He raised his voice as Mike came out of his tent. 'Taken quite a fancy to young Tandouris.

Luckily for him his only competition's a derelict cook and a mob of fat bullocks.'

'Jealous,' said Mike. 'Just because you're too old to do anything but play cards all night.'

He dodged the flying beer can, climbed into the Moke and disappeared. The remainder of us moved into the caravan to open the new tournament season of the Flyblown Downs Bridge Club. Social bridge a speciality...

NICHOLAS

There was a new vehicle when we returned to camp next afternoon, a Toyota Land Cruiser with a blue light on its roof. Gil had taken Marion and me out to show us relevant aspects of local geography, and as we drove back into the dusty clearing he said:

'Visitors. Cops by the look of it. Tandouris has probably been making a nuisance of himself with Miranda or something.' But he sounded puzzled.

However, as he got out and saw the figure reclining in one of their easy chairs beside the van he let out a great chortle.

'Jesus Christ, it's not the proper fuzz, it's Alan!'

The man stood up, revealing a figure of medium build and very erect stance. The shortness of his hair was counterbalanced by a luxuriant moustache, trimmed symmetrically across a slightly florid face. He might have been a youngish sergeant major from the British Army, except that most of them didn't come like that any more. When he spoke, his brisk, deep voice was not inappropriate to the parade ground.

'Ah, Mr Reynolds. I've come to arrest you for illegal parking in Brisbane on at least fifty occasions that I've personally noted. I must warn you that anything you say may be taken . . . – . . . what are you pointing at?'

'The dunny's that way, mate. We try to keep the bullshit out of the rest of the camp.'

A grin broke from under the moustache.

'Jesus, but you wouldn't know it though,' he said, staring pointedly around.

'Yeah, well, it was all right until you arrived. Is there any beer left, or is that expecting too much?'

'I wouldn't know, the fridge is padlocked. Inhospitable bastards!'

'That must have been Mike this morning. Sensible lad. Can't be too careful these days, with the sort of riff-raff that comes into camps when people are out. Too bad you haven't got time to stop for a beer now.'

'Well, I guess I could stretch it a bit longer. I haven't had tea yet.'

'I was afraid of that. Anyway, meet our new arrivals, Marion and Nicholas. They're Poms, but they're on the way to learning to be locals. This is Alan Campbell, who for some inexplicable reason is employed as an inspector by the Queensland Police. They obviously don't know what I know about him from our schooldays together. I sometimes wonder if I shouldn't tell them.'

'Yeah, you do that. And I'll tell them about your school career. We could share the same cell afterwards.'

The ritual slanging match was terminated by the entry of the Mini-Moke into the car park. The roof contraption was raised, revealing it to be a sort of aerial trawl net; as the vehicle came to a halt Mike pulled a lever to close the mouth of the net, then hopped out and removed a plastic container from the tapered end.

'There's a gentleman from the police here to see you, Mike,' said Gil. 'There's been a complaint from Miranda Downs.'

'I never touched her,' said Mike. 'We spent the whole night playing bridge.'

But Alan Campbell wasn't listening. He was busy removing cans of beer and several enormous T-bone steaks from an Esky cold-box in his wagon. The group broke up to shower and change, and reassembled afterwards to drink beer round a fire on which a number of steaks were now sizzling.

'So what brings you to this part of the world?' asked Gil. 'The pleasure of our company?'

'No, that's a bonus. Or something. No, I'm up here investigating a murder. Young girl at Ironbark Creek.'

Once again I felt a clutching sensation in my innards. Gil turned towards me.

'That sounds like it might be your friend. What was her name?'

'Anna Ioannides,' I replied.

'Good God, did you know her?' Alan was staring at me quite intently, with a frown.

'I never actually met her.' I explained what Fergus had told me, and then mentioned that Gil had some maggots that might have been from her body.

'Oh, they've arrived, have they?' said Alan. 'What was the score?'

'No score yet. I haven't had time to look at them. Too busy coping with visitors' – he winked at Marion – 'some of whom were unexpected and uninvited. I'll get them done in the morning for you.'

'No hurry, really. I don't suppose they'll provide any more clues than the rest of our investigations.' He sounded gloomy. 'I hate these cases where there's nothing to get your teeth into.'

'You mean the site wasn't loaded with clues?'

'Bugger all. Even one tiny scrap of evidence would've been nice. She was found without clothing under a heap of loose earth. She was killed by strangulation, apparently manual. She had some cuts and quite a few bruises on her body suggesting a struggle, and there were some other marks that looked more like gouges or tears in the flesh – cause unknown at this stage. She probably died four or five days before she was found. At least that was what the doctor worked out from the state of decomposition – your maggots might give us a closer estimate.'

'No footprints or tyre marks around the spot?'

'Oh yeah,' said Alan bitterly. 'There were plenty of prints. A whole mob of bloody cattle walked over the area just before she was found. Hoofprints galore. She was found by a geriatric stockman who heard nothing, saw nothing and knows nothing. I reckon that if the murder had been committed under his nose he wouldn't have noticed. He's so slow that if you ask him a question you may as well come back next week for the answer. He was sure that cattle duffers were responsible, but I soon discovered that in his book cattle duffers are responsible for anything and everything. He's paranoid.'

'What are cattle duffers?' asked Marion.

'Cattle thieves. What the Americans call rustlers. It's one of the growth industries up here these days, and it's bloody hard to stop. They operate at all levels in areas like this, from the little local guy up to the well-organised professionals. Some of the resulting meat'll go to local butchers who aren't too fussy about provenance, but the big guys'll usually have an unofficial contract with an unscrupulous meatworks.' His face took on a sour expression. 'I don't doubt that quite a bit of it finishes up at the factory of Miss Ioannides' father.'

'Perhaps she could have been killed by them then? Gone to make a rendezvous for her father, and one of them got carried away or something?'

'By all accounts Miss Ioannides hated her father's guts. I can't see her acting as his agent – more likely she'd have been dobbing him in. But I don't really think that's a possibility either. She was apparently bumming around the north, and I reckon she probably picked the wrong person to hitch a ride with. And that sort of crime's very hard to solve unless someone saw the vehicle parked at the spot while the victim was being raped or murdered or concealed or whatever.'

'And nobody did?'

'Not that we can find. As I said, the stockman wouldn't know whether it was arseholes or breakfast time, and nobody in the town seems to have been anywhere near Coolabah Creek for months. That's where she was found.'

'Is there a policeman at Ironbark Creek?'

'Yeah, but he's not much use. He's the main cattle duffer in the district as far as I can make out. He used to be in the Rockhampton force, and there was an investigation into some rather nasty corruption. The son of a very senior policeman was also involved, and as a result this guy was transferred to Ironbark Creek instead of being given the bullet altogether. More's the pity.'

'Did any strangers visit the town about the time she's thought to have been killed?'

'Nobody can remember any. There's one hotel there, if you can call it that, and according to its register nobody had stayed there around the time of Miss Ioannides' death. I'm not surprised – it's a wonder that anyone ever stays there. I did for my first two days in the town, till I booked out and started sleeping in the wagon. The beds are horsehair on sagging frames, and the walls must be made of cardboard. I was woken up on the second night by a truckie staggering into the next bedroom from the bar at two o'clock, belching all night, and at intervals rolling to the edge of the bed to piss over the floor. That gives you an idea of the types that visit Ironbark Creek and its hostelry. The licensing hours never get enforced because the policeman likes his beer, and the publican probably gives him a cut of the profit from the extra trading. And the hotel's laundry arrangements are a gem. The morning I was leaving I saw the old biddy who helps run the place take the sheets off my bed, hang them on the line, play a hose on them for a moment, and then leave 'em to dry. Good, eh?'

Mike was serving the steaks, accompanied once again by potatoes from the fire. I had to pass again, because now I had a sharp pain in the gut and something was obviously wrong. It seemed that my inability to eat the previous night wasn't just squeamishness after all.

As we were eating, Frank suddenly asked:

'If you only found a naked body, how on earth did you identify it as Anna Ioannides?'

'It took us a little while, but that was our one stroke of luck. The surgeon doing the post mortem discovered that she belonged to a scarce blood group – don't ask me how they can still tell such a thing when the body's half way putrid but they can. We prayed that she might have been a blood donor and asked the blood banks around Australia for names of any females in the broad age range with that blood group. We got fifty-three names and addresses and we managed to find forty-six of them alive and well. We started chasing dental records for the other seven, and Miss Ioannides turned up as the third. She'd had some dental work done, and there was a perfect match. She'd been a regular blood donor at the Sydney University sessions.'

Gil said: 'I'm not asking this for prurient reasons, but had she been raped?'

'Not as far as we know. The surgeon said there might have been signs of sexual activity but he couldn't be positive, and Dr O'Riordan's told us that the girl led an active sex life. There was no indication of abnormal violence of that sort, or mutilation or anything. Just a probable fight followed by strangulation. God only knows why – there can be so many causes.'

There was silence for a while, then Gil spoke again.

'I'm still puzzled by the naked body. If she was just killed after a fight, wouldn't the person who did it have dumped her as quickly as possible and got the hell out of it before someone came along? Why hang around and undress her?'

Alan shrugged. 'To avoid having her identified, perhaps. Maybe that was more of a risk than hanging around. After all, the murderer took the trouble to bury the body as well.'

'Did you find the clothes?'

'No, not a trace. We scoured the area thoroughly and found nothing but hoofprints and cow turds.' He was looking gloomy again.

'So you don't know whether she was actually killed at Coolabah Creek or merely dumped there?

'No, not even that. I'm thinking of changing my job for an easier one, like brain surgery.'

'Where do you intend to go from here, then?'

'Round the bend, most probably. No, I thought I might just wait for your report on the maggots, and then go to Townsville which was the last place from which she made contact with anyone that we know of, and see if I can pick up any trace of her – where she lived, who her friends were, and so on. It's possible that it was someone from there who killed her and then dumped her later out here in the bush, though it's a hell of a long way to bring her. There'd have been remote spots much closer to Townsville.'

'Well,' said Gil, 'have another beer and forget about it till morning. Tomorrow I promise you I'll find you a dramatically exciting clue amongst the maggots!'

He probably didn't believe the exciting bit any more than Alan did. But it turned out to be true.

* * *

I had a pretty uncomfortable night, much of it spent trotting back and forth to the dunny as they called it, where my bowels discharged thin liquid with wracking spasms. The mild anti-diarrhoea capsules I'd brought with me weren't working, and by morning I had to admit that medical treatment seemed desirable.

'Hm,' said Gil, pondering for a while. 'There's not much of that around these parts. We could always call the Flying

Doctor, of course, but seeing that Alan's going to Townsville I'd suggest that you go along with him. You can find a doctor there easily, and it'll be a more civilised place for recuperating than here. When you're okay again you can take the Mount Isa train as far as Hughenden, and if you give us a call first either Marion or I can pick you up from the station there.'

In my weakening state I thought getting back a bit closer to civilisation was a pretty good idea, and I went to pack some clothes. I stowed my bag in Alan's vehicle, and we sat down to wait while Gil processed the sample of larvae from Anna Ioannides.

It took a lot longer than anyone had expected, and when Gil finally came out of the caravan there was an odd expression on his face.

'Alan, old son, I've got your result, but I don't think you're going to like me.'

'I might have known you'd come up with something stupid, you bastard. Okay, let's have it. Was she murdered around here or somewhere else?'

'The body must have lain in rainforest for at least a short while, so definitely somewhere else.'

'Oh Jesus, there's no rainforest for hundreds of miles from here, and there's none at Townsville either, which was my best lead. You bastard! There's hundreds of patches of rainforest up and down the coast – can't you narrow it down a bit?'

'As a matter of fact I can,' said Gil, 'but that's the bit you aren't going to like. It must have been in Papua New Guinea...'

* * *

In the stunned silence that followed, the birdsong around the camp seemed particularly loud.

Finally Alan spoke. 'Bloody hell, Gil, I thought you were supposed to be good at this. That's bloody ridiculous. It's impossible! She was last seen in Townsville, for Christ's sake.'

'There are regular flights from Townsville to Port Moresby. She could have taken one.'

'Yeah, okay, I wasn't thinking of that. It's the return journey that doesn't add up. There's no rainforest around Port Moresby. It's bloody dreary dry savanna like around Townsville. So she was taken elsewhere in PNG, and then what? She was murdered, left out for a while, and then someone decides to take her to Ironbark Creek. Your average commercial flight doesn't usually accept decomposing bodies as luggage, so he or she would have had to have a boat on standby, get the body on to the boat, sail to somewhere in northern Australia where they had land transport also available, and then drive all the way to Ironbark Creek, which as you may have noticed is a long way from the coast. The whole operation would have taken days. And why, for Christ's sake? Why not just leave the body in PNG?'

'I did say you weren't going to like it,' said Gil.

'It's not a matter of not liking it, it's bloody impossible! You must be wrong. How can you be so sure that it's PNG? Maggots covered in bird of paradise feathers or something?'

'No, but the male ones were all wearing penis sheaths.... Listen, if you want to doubt me, that's your business, but at least do it on informed opinion. Come inside and I'll give you a crash course on maggot anatomy, and then you can judge the reliability of the evidence. Then you can go back to Townsville and work out how she was brought back from PNG.'

'Okay, I'll do it, if only to prove you wrong,' said Alan.

They went into the laboratory caravan, and Marion and I decided to tag along. It was a biological problem such as we'd never encountered before, and nobody seemed to object when we hung around.

'Okay,' said Gil. 'You'll be like the average lay person who thinks that all maggots look alike.'

'Yeah, white, squashy and disgusting. Good fish bait.'

'Yes, well, once more your ignorance is displayed to the world. Come over here and look at this specimen under the microscope. Right, there are two ends – one sharp end, one blunt end. The sharp end is the front, the blunt end is the back. The sharp end has two little black hooks, right?'

Alan peered through the twin eyepieces. 'Right,' he said, grudgingly.

'They're the mouth-hooks, which are used for feeding. Highly trained experts like me, and probably anyone other than thick police officers, can tell a lot about the maggots' diet and hence their habits from the shapes of the hooks. Cow dung maggots have flat spatulas for shovelling in the wet stuff, blowfly maggots have ones like butchers' knives for slicing off the meat, plant feeding maggots have little saws for rasping plant tissue, and my favourites are the predacious ones.'

His eyes had lit up by this stage.

'They have thin mouth-hooks shaped like sickles and very sharp. They slash down into their prey, then turn them outwards to lock into the victim. Then they use a couple of accessory pieces shaped like drills to enlarge the hole, into which they pour their digestive juices.'

'Aw, pull the other one. I'm not as stupid as you seem to think.'

'This is all fair dinkum. You can read it in that book over there.'

'Maybe. What's it all got to do with Miss Ioannides, anyway?'

'Not much,' said Gil grinning. 'I just thought you might to learn something really interesting. Okay, back to the stiffs. Miss Ioannides' maggots have slicing mouth-hooks like typical blowflies. The key area for them is the flat end at the back, but I'll have to give you a bit of background on that first.'

He slid open a small drawer containing microscope slides and put one under the microscope.

'Look at this specimen which is the back end of a maggot, turned upwards to show the hind spiracles. You'll see two round blackish plates.'

We all took turns to peer this time.

'Right, they're the spiracles through which the maggot breathes. There are two long tracheae or air tubes inside the spiracle, running the length of the body. Each one opens at a small anterior spiracle just behind the head, which probably doesn't do much because the head's buried in gunk most of the time, and then each tube opens at the back end through one of those plates. The maggot pokes its back end out to the fresh air every so often, and draws in oxygen before it goes down again.'

'So?'

'Okay, look again now that I've increased the magnification' – he rotated a ring on the body of the microscope – 'and you'll see one round hole and three long straight slits in each plate. The round hole's called the button. It's not actually an air hole but a scar left after the last moult, but its position on the plate can be important for identification. It's the slits that are the actual holes through which the air goes in and out. Depending on the fly family they can be straight, or arc-like, or wiggly in all sorts of patterns, or just a mass of small holes. It's their shape that's the clincher for identification, and in the case of virtually all blowflies they're pretty straight.'

'Yeah, I can see these ones are long and straight,' said Alan. 'They look like they've got little trees growing out of them, too.'

'Smart lad, we'll make an entomologist out of you yet. They're the perispiracular glands, but you knew that of course. They actually come out of little holes just beside the slits, and down the holes are glands that secrete water-repellent fluid.'

'You're getting unreal again...'

'Well, if you'd been submerged in festering corpse juices and you came up for air, you wouldn't get very far if your air holes were clogged up with garbage. If you watch a maggot come up for air, as soon as it hits the open air the back end clears like magic. Courtesy of the perispiracular glands.'

'Fascinating. You must make a TV documentary sometime. Should go down really well around dinnertime. So what's all this to do with Miss Ioannides, though?'

'Let me put one of her maggots back under the scope.' He fished a fat white larva out of a well-stuffed tube, and put it in the dish under the microscope beside the other one. 'You remember the previous maggot had straight slits. Well, look at these.'

Alan looked down the eyepieces. 'Very elegant, I will say. They're really curled around. They'd make quite a good wallpaper design.'

'Pretty, aren't they? There are only two lots of blowflies known to have slits like that. One is the tumbu fly of Africa, where the maggot lives under the skin of living animals in a sort of blister, and the other's *Calliphora aiyurensis*, a large orange blowfly from around Aiyura and certain other rainforest habitats in Papua New Guinea. You can thank your lucky stars that at least I'm not claiming that Miss Ioannides was killed in Africa.'

Alan just rolled his eyes at Gil, who went on: 'There are four confirmatory features which make the PNG ID the most likely. The buttons are nearer the bottom of each plate than in any other species. The perispiracular gland hairs are much more branched than in any other species. Then there are the anterior spiracles, which aren't usually of much use but in this case they are. Each one has tiny holes that are set on little lobes or fingers, and these spiracles only have four lobes each. That's very unusual in a blowfly – there are usually ten, fifteen, twenty or more. And finally there are bands of tiny spines around the body which the maggot uses for getting purchase to move on slimy surfaces. The shapes of the spines and the patterns of the bands are pretty characteristic too. So you're stuck with it, I'm afraid.'

'What a bastard,' said Alan. 'Are you sure it couldn't occur in Australian rainforest as well?'

'Well, we've collected the rainforests pretty well, right up to Cairns and Mossman, and it's never turned up yet. With the amount of dead meat I've put out all over the place I would have thought I'd have found it by now if it was there, but I suppose there is a slight chance.' He didn't sound convinced.

'I knew I shouldn't have come to this dump. My mother warned me about associating with people like you.'

'So you'll be looking forward to my evidence in court, then?'

'Yeah. Don't ring us, we'll call you. Maybe.' He paused. 'If by any chance we did need your evidence, even though I'd rather forget all about it at the moment, would you be able to testify as an expert in court?'

'I've been going from a scientific paper description in what I told you. I've never seen *Calliphora aiyurensis* maggots first-hand before. To be able to testify with suitable authority I should have compared them to some specimens in a known collection.' He grinned at Alan. 'The only trouble is that I'm running low on travel funds. But of course the police would be funding the trip, wouldn't they?'

'Jesus, you bastard. I can just see the Commissioner when I front him for a free holiday for Reynolds in PNG. He'll have me laid out like an anatomy demonstration, with various bits missing.'

'PNG would be nice, but I was thinking of Melbourne, actually. They've got a good reference collection at the National Museum of Victoria of stuff like that from PNG.'

'Ah, well, that might be a bit easier to justify. Actually, if you're going down there at our expense you could do a job for me too. You could go and chat to old man Ioannides, the girl's father. The Victorian police interviewed him, and they got bugger all. But it's never the same when it's not your case. There's all sorts of protocol procedures if I do an official investigation inter-state, but there's nothing to stop you.'

'That's fair enough. Anything for an old mate. Which should I stay at, do you think – the Hilton or the Hyatt...?'

'Old Mother Bailey's bed and breakfast's about all we'll pay you for. But then you earn so much you'll be able to upgrade, won't you?'

Gil made an impolite gesture with his middle finger.

'Well,' said Alan. 'I'd better be getting young Nicholas to the quack in Townsville. Ready?'

We put our bags in the back of the police wagon and drove off, leaving Marion alone with Gil.

NICHOLAS

Alan Campbell deposited me at Flanagan's Hotel, and then left to organise further investigations with the aid of the Townsville police. I lay down on the bed in a freshly painted room, and immediately felt better than I had at Flyblown Downs. Flanagan's was an old city pub, plain and wood-panelled with a creaking wooden balcony at the front. It wasn't the best the city could offer, but it was conveniently near the surgery of a doctor recommended by the Townsville police surgeon and the rooms were comfortable enough.

Next morning I went to see the doctor who provisionally diagnosed an infestation of intestinal flagellates. 'Asking for it in a country like that,' he'd said rather sniffily when I mentioned the stopover in Thailand, and he prescribed some tablets in anticipation of the pathology tests on the sample that I'd had to produce. I wasn't sure about a Thailand connection because that had been a couple of weeks earlier, but maybe the parasites had a long incubation period. Whatever, I just wanted to get right again.

I went back to my bed in the hotel, as I was still a bit wobbly.

The ceiling fan made a slow, soothing swish overhead. I pulled up the light sheet which was the only covering on the bed, and settled down to read a P.D. James novel that I'd found in a bookshop near the hotel. I looked at the picture of the author on the back cover and thought that she reminded me of one of my PhD examiners. At the viva this woman had looked at me with the same hooded eyes and ironic smile as in the cover photo, confirming my worst fears about the quality of my thesis. I was then very surprised later when I'd had to make relatively few amendments for the thesis to pass.

This twinge of uncomfortable reminiscence served to heighten my anticipation of the book, and I settled down for what looked like a good read...

I woke again at the sound of the door opening. A female figure was entering backwards, dragging a vacuum cleaner. My fingers fumbled at the book that had half slipped from my grasp, and at the sound the figure turned.

'Aw Jeez, I'm sorry, sir! I didn't know there was anyone still here.' She peered at me, frowning. 'You all right? You look awful white, you know.'

She must have been in her early twenties, of indeterminate figure under a loose cleaning smock.

'I'm a bit sick, actually. I've just been to see the doctor and he told me to go back to bed. You'd better come in and do the room because I'm afraid I'll be here all day.'

The girl looked at me very doubtfully, perhaps wondering whether she should disturb me or maybe wondering what she might catch. However, she pulled the vacuum cleaner into the room and went back to get scouring powder, dusters and clean sheets.

'Here, you'd better let me do the bed first and then you can lie down again.' She whizzed the sheets off and substituted fresh ones with practised deftness. I stood in the very short pyjamas that I'd bought in Sydney, feeling more like a beanpole than ever. Then I climbed gratefully back into the cool, dry bed while the girl dusted, vacuumed, and cleaned my washbasin.

'Anything else I can get you while I'm here?' she asked as she finished.

'I wouldn't mind a cup of coffee. Have one yourself if you like.' I nodded at the electric jug and the sachets on a shelf beside the washbasin.

The girl looked very doubtful. 'I'm not supposed to do that . . . oh, stuff it, I'd love one! The manager's out and I'm ahead this morning. Don't tell anyone, though, for Christ's sake.'

I shook my head, and watched her filling the jug. She had to bail the water in with the glass from the washbasin because the jug wouldn't fit under the tap, like in so many hotels. She looked away from me while the jug heated, maybe being a little embarrassed.

'Black and no sugar for me,' I said, and she brought it over to me. She perched decorously on the end of the bed with hers, since the only chair in the room was covered with my clothes.

We sat in silence drinking our coffees, and I began to wish I was a better conversationalist. I was an only son, educated at an all-male school, and I often had trouble making small talk to the opposite sex, especially one whose world revolved around being a chambermaid. But the thought of that job suddenly gave me an idea.

'I don't suppose you remember meeting a girl called Anna Ioannides, do you?'

'No.' The girl showed neither recognition nor interest. 'Should I?'

'She used to be a chambermaid at a Townsville hotel – I don't know which. I just thought you might have come across her.'

'Name doesn't ring a bell. There's quite a lot of hotels in Townsville.'

I opened my bedside drawer and took out my wallet. I pulled out a picture of Anna that Alan had given me two days earlier, and passed it to the girl.

'Oh, her! Yeah, I have met her once or twice. She used to work at the Grand along with a mate o' mine, Raelene. The mad rooter, we used to call her, because she was always having it off with men. Got chucked out for it in the end. But her name wasn't what you said, it was Marie Johnson.'

'Do you know what happened to her?'

'Nah, haven't seen her for a while. I only met her a coupla times at a disco and a beach party. Raelene might know.' She looked harder at Nicholas. 'Why are you interested in her, anyway?' She edged back on the bed a little, thinking perhaps that I was keen on mad rooters.

'She was a friend of my brother-in-law – used to work for him in Sydney. She wrote to him from Townsville and said she was working as a chambermaid, and then he didn't hear any more from her. When he heard I was coming up here he asked me to look her up.'

'Oh.' The girl didn't volunteer any more than that, so I tried again.

'Do you think I might meet your friend Raelene to ask her?'

'Dunno. I'll let her know you're interested if I see her.' The girl seemed to be hedging, which was curious. I hoped it was only because she was uncomfortable talking to guests like this, and I thought I'd better not press further at this stage. I could always visit the Grand Hotel later anyway.

We finished our coffee and the girl washed the cups. She wheeled out the vacuum cleaner, then returned with a large handful of extra coffee sachets for me. She winked at me, and departed with the rest of the cleaning materials.

I lay back on the bed and pondered. I wondered what P.D. James would have been making of it all. A great deal more than I was, for sure, but I did still feel rather weak. Perhaps tomorrow I'd feel stronger. I picked up the book and started again on Chapter One.

* * *

Next morning I was feeling marginally better, though not as much as I'd hoped. I wasn't due to receive the pathology results from the doctor for another day, so I decided to stay in bed. At twenty to eleven the girl came to clean the room again, this time knocking gingerly and asking if she might. I offered her coffee once more, but she declined saying that the manager was around and she'd be out on her ear if he caught her. However, she boiled the jug for me while she was cleaning the washbasin.

As she brought the cup of coffee to me she hesitated, then said:

'I saw Raelene last night. She said she'd like to talk to you about Marie.'

'Oh, that's great,' I replied. 'I can pop round to the Grand to see her when I'm better.'

The girl hesitated again.

'Well . . . actually she said she'd like to see you as soon as possible. She doesn't want to come up here because people would talk, but she wondered if you could make it to the park on the Strand at six o'clock tonight? It's only just round the corner from here – I said I thought you might just be up to that.'

She looked unhappy at having to put the hard word on a sick man like that, but her friend must have impressed some urgency on her. I was puzzled at what possible reasons there could be for that, but clearly the request couldn't be ignored.

'Of course I can manage it,' I replied, trying to convince myself as much as anyone. 'Will you be coming too?'

'No, I've got to get home to my dad.'

'So how do I find her?'

'You walk down the street that runs along the side of this hotel. Crace Street, it's called. A hundred metres or so you'll get to the Strand. It's a wide street with lots of coconut palms. Just across it there's a gate into a park, and the path leads up to a rotunda. She'll be on the bench in the rotunda, and she'll be there by six. She's about my height and build. Better looking, though,' she added a little wistfully, as she left the room.

At five thirty I got up and showered. By ten to six I wished I was back in bed again, but I knew where my duty lay so I wandered off to the Strand. I found it just as described, until I got to the rotunda bench on which were seated two elderly derelicts swigging in turn from a bottle. I peered around until I saw a figure under some nearby trees, waving. I went over.

'Are you Raelene?'

'Yeh. Just my bloody luck the methos were there. Come on, let's go and sit on the sea wall and talk.'

I looked at her as we walked across the grass. The girl in the hotel was right, Raelene was attractive. She had a pertly pretty face, a short, boyish haircut, a T-shirt with nothing on under it, and tight jeans that must have been most uncomfortable in the tropical heat. She also had too much make-up, and a touch of harshness. I thought the girl in the hotel had seemed nicer.

We sat down on the stone wall at the edge of the beach, and Raelene spoke.

'Something's happened to her, hasn't it?' She seemed unsure of herself, or uneasy.

'Why do you think that?' I asked, trying not to sound too inquisitorial.

'You a cop?' she snapped back.

'No, I promise you that. I'm just a friend of a friend, as I told your mate at Flanagan's. Tell me what you think might have happened to her, and I'll say if you're right or not.'

Raelene shrugged petulantly. 'It was just the people she used to mix with – I didn't like them,' she said dismissively.

I'm normally a patient sort of a person, but at the moment I still felt sick and I didn't feel like pussyfooting around.

'She's been murdered,' I said bluntly. 'Somebody strangled her and dumped her body in the outback.'

'Oh Christ, no!' whispered the girl, looking at me in horror. 'Christ, no...'

She stared at the ground in silence, and I simply waited. It came in a moment or two.

'I told her she was a bloody fool to mix with them. I told her but she wouldn't bloody listen. Oh Christ, the stupid, bloody fool...'

'Who did you tell her not to mix with?' I asked, a bit more gently this time.

'The crowd at the disco,' she said wearily. 'There was a group that went there regularly. They used to get up to all sorts of things, shoplifting and that. Well, I didn't mind that so much, but they used to pass round joints at the disco, and worse. Drugs scare the shit out of me, but Marie just thought it was all a joke. She used to go and chat them up, puff away at the bongs, and then come and tell me it was great. She used to say I was worrying about nothing – didn't know how to live and all that crap. Shit, how could she have been so bloody stupid?'

She was dabbing at her eyes, and the make-up was running slightly.

'She was an adult and free to do what she wanted. You could have just let her get on with it...'

'I liked her a lot. She was a good mate,' said the girl piteously. 'I felt real sorry for her too. She was screwed up about fellers, and they gave her a hard time. Bloody men,' she added vindictively.

'I heard she lost her job through relationships with men. Found in bed with one of the guests or something?'

'It wasn't as straightforward as that,' said Raelene bitterly. 'The manager caught her at it with a guest. It was just after working hours, but you're not allowed to do it with guests at any time. But he wasn't going to sack her. He said she could stay on as long as he had his bit as well. I dunno exactly what she said to him but it must have been pretty bad. I saw him just afterwards and he was white with rage. He threw Marie straight out and wouldn't even let her get her things – he had them sent after her. I saw her again the same night. She thought that was all a big joke too. She said she was fed up with cleaning up other people's dirty rooms and she was going to move in more exciting circles. That was the last time I saw her.' She was sniffing a bit and swallowing.

The prospects are opening up, I thought. An angry and spurned hotel manager and some dubious "friends" of Anna's.

'Do you think by "exciting circles" she meant the disco crowd?'

'Dunno, she never said.'

'Do you know who they are?'

'Not really. I know one or two first names, that's all.'

'I should be able to contact them then, if I went along to the disco?'

She looked me up and down, pursing her lips. 'Not in gear like that. They'd laugh you out of the place. Listen, you're never going to look trendy enough. The person you want to talk to is Vic, who's the assistant manager at the disco. Vic knows all the people and all the names. You wanna go in the morning, when they're cleaning up and it isn't so crazy.'

'Where do I find the place?'

'It's called Screwball. It's in Hermit Park. You'll find it in the phone book.'

I suddenly found that my head was beginning to swirl. I think the lack of food was catching up with me.

'Thanks a lot for all your help. If I need to ask you anything else I'll know where to contact you.'

The girl gave me an oblique look. Not if I have anything to do with it, the eyes said. And she was gone.

GIL REYNOLDS

I made it to Victoria, courtesy of the grudging support of the Queensland Police, but that was about the only positive part. I'd arrived at the National Museum of Victoria to find that the fly expert I'd intended to meet had just left on a month's collecting trip in far north Queensland, where I'd just come from. Sod's Law proved yet again. The expert was due to start at Normanton, pass quite close to Flyblown Downs, and continue up the Cape York Peninsula almost to its tip. So all I'd been able to do was search the museum collection for maggots like Alan's, but if they were there I couldn't locate them. I did, however, manage to pinch some packing material to send some of my specimens to the other expert in Konedobu, for direct comparison with the Papua New Guinea specimens. I also had a quick look in the Museum library at the original published description, which made me somewhat more convinced that my larvae may be the same as the PNG species.

Having largely failed in that part of my mission I thought at least I'd better get something out of Nicos Ioannides, or Alan Campbell would want his money back. I telephoned the meat processing works.

'Good afternoon, Hellenic Meat Processing Proprietary Limited, may I help you?'

'Good afternoon. I'd like to speak to Mr Ioannides' private secretary, please.'

'Mr Ioannides' *private* secretary?' The tone suggested that I'd just made an indecent suggestion.

'Yes please.'

A pause. 'I'll see if she's free.' Frost emanated from the phone earpiece.

Christ, I thought, it's only his secretary I'm after...

Click, click, silence, click.

'Hullo,' said the telephonist.

'Hullo.'

'Oh, you're still there.' Disappointment mingled with the frost. 'Is it important?'

'Yes. Very.'

'Oh,' said the telephonist. 'I'll see if I can get her to speak to you, then. One moment please.'

More clicks.

'Hullo,' said a deeper female voice, abruptly.

'Hullo. Are you Mr Ioannides' personal secretary?'

'Yes.' Snappy.

Stay polite, I thought – don't let her rattle you. 'My name is Dr Gilbert Reynolds. I'm a Queensland research scientist and I also happen to be a friend of the policeman who is investigating the death of Mr Ioannides' daughter. He asked if when I was in Melbourne I could call on Mr Ioannides to put a few questions on his behalf. I wondered if I might make an appointment, please?'

'Mr Ioannides is a very busy man.'

'Yes, but surely this is important?' Staying unrattled was getting difficult. 'I'm doing this at the request of the police!'

'Mr Ioannides has already been interviewed by the police.'

'Yes, but that was the Victorian police who weren't actually working on the case.'

'I'm sure Mr Ioannides has great faith in the Victorian Police.'

'Oh, for God's sake! Kindly put me on to him and let me ask him myself!'

'Mr Ioannides is a very busy man. However, as you are so insistent I will enquire from him.'

A pause.

'Hullo?' came the female voice again.

'Hullo.'

'Mr Ioannides informs me that he has already made a statement to the police, and he has nothing further to add to this. Good afternoon!'

Click.

I was livid by this stage, not only at the waste of my time and Alan's money but also at the rudeness of Hellenic Meats. It was Ioannides' own daughter, for God's sake. Didn't he care anything about catching her killer?

A drink was becoming increasingly desirable, preferably in better company than the most recent. I tried to think of someone I knew in Melbourne who might be accessible and prepared to have a yarn over a few beers. No names sprang immediately to mind, until the thought of meat processing reminded me of Bill Bowman. I glanced at my watch, rushed back to the phone booth, looked up the Department of Health and dialled.

'Hullo, Australian Department of Health.'

'Hullo, may I speak to Mr Bill Bowman, please.'

'I'll try, sir, but he may have gone by now.'

My heart sank even further.

Clicks and a pause, then: 'I'm afraid he doesn't seem to be ... hang on a moment, he's just going through the door.' I could hear a great shout in the background of "Mr Bowman!", then: 'He's just coming, sir.'

'G'day, Bowman here.'

'G'day, you old bastard. Gil Reynolds here. I'm in Melbourne and in bad need of a drink. What do you propose to do about it?'

'Dunno. Meet me over a beer and I'll think about it. Where are you?'

'Just outside the National Museum of Victoria at the moment.'

Good! Don't move and I'll be past the front door in about ten minutes. Watch for a white EH Holden with a ding in the side. See ya.'

It was going to be interesting to see what Bill would have to say about all this. One thing was sure, he would certainly have something to say.

* * *

We settled on a rather out of the way pub, where Bill said the beer was good and there'd be less disturbance for a chat.

'Too many yuppies grogging on after work in the city pubs – you can't hear yourself think in most of 'em. So what brings you down to civilisation, old son?'

'I was hoping to identify a maggot, but the local expert at

the National Museum's just left on a trip to outback Queensland – to exactly where I've just come from, as it happens – and the technician didn't know where the relevant maggots were stored. Bit of a bugger really.'

'I know you've been up to some pretty revolting things in the past. What's the particular interest in this one?'

'It's a forensic one. In fact you may know the father of the person who was killed – Nicos Ioannides. From what I've heard he's sailed very close to the wind in relation to various regulations.'

'Including Health, I'd have to say. But who was it – not his wild daughter?'

'It was Anna. From what little I've heard it sounds as though she was a bit wild, so I guess that's who you mean.'

'Anna, yeah. I only met her the once. Strong character – takes after her father in that, but the two of them were apparently at daggers drawn all the time.'

'I'm actually down here at the Queensland Police's expense. There's a special reason for needing this particular maggot identified, but they also asked me to talk to Nicos Ioannides about the murder. The Victorian Police interviewed him, but they didn't have any of the detailed background on the case and they didn't get anything of help at all. But when I contacted his meat company I got the bum's rush, very rudely. Through his private secretary – he wouldn't talk to me directly – he refused to see me, said he'd been interviewed by the Vic Police and he had nothing to add. Since he didn't know what I might have been able to say, that was a load of crap. I don't know whether he was deliberately trying to conceal something, or whether he's just a bloody-minded, obstreperous bastard generally.'

'Jeez, they obviously did give you a rough time. He certainly is a hard and obstreperous bugger. Whether he might have something to hide, I couldn't say. At least in relation to his daughter, that is – when it comes to his meat works and his operations there's definitely a great deal to hide. Unfortunately for us, he's pretty good at hiding it and we're only rarely able to pin anything on him. But what was so special about this particular maggot?'

'Anna Ioannides' body was found near the edge of Coolabah Creek, which is not all that far from Ironbark Creek in the Gulf Country. The whole area's dry as a desert rat's bum. The body contained quite a large number of maggots, all of which are of a type only known from rainforest in Papua New Guinea. Sounds like a remarkable conjuring trick somewhere, but nobody yet can explain how that could happen. I urgently need a sample of the PNG larvae to compare to Anna's, and there were supposed to be some here. In desperation I've just sent some of my samples on to PNG to see if they could do a comparison, but I don't know if they've got a larval expert at the moment.'

'Hm, I'm glad I'm only working on animal quarantine problems. They're tricky enough, but not as curly as that one. If the body was exposed in PNG and then brought to Australia there'd be quarantine implications from that too, but it's hard to see a possible time frame. It'd take quite a few days from start to when she was found, and my memory is that the maggots would probably already have pupated at your sort of temperatures.'

'Yeah, that's one of the problems, and the other is the sheer logistics of what apparently happened. It takes a bit of effort to cart a corpse over large distances, including over the sea.'

'Well, one of the experts at efficient long haulage of carcases is Nicos Ioannides, of course – he does it all the time with cattle. But it would be a hell of a thing to suggest that he killed his own daughter or had her killed and then dumped, and anyway why do it in PNG? And if it was indeed done there, why not just leave the body there? Why bring it back to Australia?'

'Fortunately I'm not the cop who's got to solve this one, but he's a mate of mine from old days, Alan Campbell, and he's relying on me to come up with at least an idea or two.'

'So did you say that you were up near Ironbark Creek anyway?'

'Yeah, I'm actually doing a survey that has quarantine implications. I'm collecting as many different larvae from northern Queensland as I can. You'd know that often it's larvae that turn up somewhere with quarantine significance rather than adult flies, and it can take a while to breed out the adults for identification. And sometimes they die before they hatch out too. So the idea is that you don't have to wait for adults – you can have a simple guide to all the known larvae that are native or already introduced in the north, and then anything new can be picked up immediately. After this I'll be trying to do a parallel guide to the larvae of nasties that are found in surrounding countries but aren't here yet. Things like screwworm in PNG, various sorts of fruit flies, and so on.'

'So you're not just a useless bastard after all?'

'Depends who you ask. Right now my mate the detective inspector certainly thinks I am. He's not at all happy with PNG as the source of his larvae.'

NICHOLAS

I was feeling frustrated at not being able to do more, but I did feel a little better and I decided to go and find Vic to ask about Anna. I went down to the hotel reception.

'Excuse me, I think there's a suburb here called Hermit Park. What would be the best way to get there from here?'

'Well, you can take a cab – there's a rank just down the road. But if you aren't in a hurry there's also a bus and it's cheaper. Route 43, and it goes from the bus stop just opposite our front entrance.'

'Thanks. I might try the bus. Cheers.'

I went outside and crossed the road, and a 43 bus came along in about five minutes. Paying my money to the driver I said: 'I'm going to a club called Screwball when I get to Hermit Park. Would you be able to tell me where it is when we get there?'

The driver gave me a slightly odd look, but just said: 'Yair mate, no problem.'

As they drove I could see why the receptionist had said "if

you aren't in a hurry", because the bus took the scenic route – but that was actually a nice way to see a bit more of Townsville.

When we pulled up in Hermit Park the driver called out: 'See that street just on the left up the road. Go down that and Screwball's on the next corner along.'

'Thanks, mate.' I was slowly learning the language.

I wandered down and stood for a moment outside the club, looking for signs of life. There weren't any, so I went and tried the front door which was open. Inside there was a rather stale fug from people and liquor the previous evening. I was suddenly hailed from behind the counter where someone was sweeping.

'You lookin' for something?'

'I was hoping to find someone called Vic.'

'I'm Vic. Whaddaya want?'

I went over to the counter. Vic was short and had an uncompromising crew cut. She also had a large bosom which made it hard to read the slogan on her T-shirt, though in time I managed to read it as "UP YOURS!". I also noticed that on the back of the T-shirt were two fingers making a V-sign.

It wasn't the most promising start, and I thought I'd better launch straight in.

'I'm asking about someone called Anna Ioannides, who may have been known up here as Marie Johnson. I'm not a cop or anything like that. She used to work for my brother-in-law who's a good friend. She was murdered several weeks ago, and her body was found inland from here.'

Vic gasped. 'Shit, that's bloody terrible. The poor bloody girl. I told her that she was mixing with the wrong sorta people, but she just seemed to take it all as a joke.' She put her broom down. 'Christ, you've really thrown me. Do you want a cup o' coffee or something? I need to sit down for a minute.'

'Coffee'd be great thanks. Black and no sugar.'

Vic disappeared behind the bar, and reappeared in a few minutes with two cups of coffee. 'Siddown over here', she said, pointing at a table with a couple of chairs. 'So what bloody happened?'

'She was strangled, and her naked body was buried in a shallow grave near Ironbark Creek west of here. No clues at all as to who might have done it. I'm sorry if that's a bit full on, but you did ask. Me and my brother-in-law would just like to get some justice for her. We know that she was in Townsville not all that long before it happened, which is why I'm asking around here a bit now.'

I thought I'd see what the response was without saying anything about a Papua New Guinea connection.

'She was Marie up here – I didn't know her other name that you said. She was a great one for the men. She was all over them and enthusiastic for a bit, and then she suddenly went off them. She was pretty full on when she ditched them, and some of them wouldn't have liked that. But I wouldn't like to name anyone I think'd do that sort of thing to her. Knock her around a bit, maybe, but not strangle her for God's sake.'

She paused for a moment, thinking. 'There was one person who might have been worse trouble than the rest of them. I can't stand his guts, so I may as well tell you. He's the son of the mayor of Townsville, and he's a right shit. I'm pretty sure he deals in drugs, though I couldn't prove it. His dad as well as being mayor's quite a big landowner in these parts. He lives up at Mount Spec which is a bit inland about sixty or seventy k's north of here, but he's got several big cattle properties further north. One of 'em's near Iron Range – that's way up the Cape York Peninsula. I don't think he's got anything near Ironbark Creek, but. They don't go that far inland.'

'What's the son's name, by the way?'

'Wayne. Wayne Robertson.'

'And what does he do? By way of a job, I mean.'

'I dunno really. He's always flashing plenty of money around, but I've never heard of a particular job. I guess he probably helps his dad with some of the things like cattle sales, though they employ plenty of other people to do that too. But it wouldn't surprise me if a lot of the cash is pretty suss. Some of it might be from drugs, I dunno, or it might be something else. He's always trying to crack on to the women here, too, but most of 'em don't like him. I've heard he can get a bit violent, though he's not the only one to do that around here.'

'Can you remember when you last saw Marie, and what she might have been doing? Anything that might have led to what happened to her?'

'She used to be round here a lot, but then she suddenly vanished. Somebody told me that she'd gone up north – right up the peninsula, I think they said – but I can't tell you any more than that. I missed her actually – she was a good kid, just a bit screwed up. Maybe that's why she liked Screwball as a club. If you can get the bastard who done that to her, good luck to you. She never deserved that.'

'Well, I'll pass that on to my brother-in-law, and thanks for telling me all this. I hope it'll help in due course.'

'You're welcome. Maybe don't tell people too much about

me saying all that about Wayne. He's got a mean streak, and I wouldn't like to go the same way as Marie. Not that I'm saying he did it, but you never know.'

'No problem, and thanks again for what you've said. If we get anywhere I'll make sure you're one of the first to know.'

'Thanks. See ya, mate, and good luck.' She disappeared out behind the counter again, muttering: 'The stupid bloody kid, she shoulda known there's some right bastards around…'

* * *

Back in my hotel room I thought about what Vic had said. It sounded as though she'd known Anna reasonably well, and also that she had shrewd judgement of some of the other people around. I wondered if Alan Campbell was still in Townsville. When I was getting the bus to Hermit Park I'd noticed that the main Police Station was just up the street, so I went out of the hotel and into the station.

'I was wondering if Inspector Alan Campbell's here at the moment? It's Nicholas Twistleton, and I've got a bit of information relevant to his enquiry into the murder of Anna Ioannides.'

'Thank you, sir, if you just leave it with me I'll make sure he gets it.'

'I'd rather pass it on to him personally, if you don't mind. I was involved a bit when he was investigating out at Ironbark Creek, and this relates to something we discussed out there.'

There was no way I was just going to pass on the comments I'd heard to a third party.

The desk officer gave me a dirty look, but went into the back office. He came out to say: 'He's still in Townsville, and he'll be out in a minute.'

When Alan came out and saw me he said: 'G'day, mate – how about we go for a coffee down the main street?'

Outside he said: 'Anything to get out of there. They don't exactly make a copper from Brisbane welcome. Makes you wonder what they've got to hide.'

We went into the Copper Kettle and ordered coffees, then sat in the most secluded seat that we could find.

With a rather neutral expression Alan said: 'You've got some news on Anna then.'

'I remembered that Fergus said Anna had gone to Townsville and was working as a chambermaid, so when a maid came into my bedroom to clean while I was sick in bed I asked her if she knew Anna. She didn't know the name at all, but when I showed her a photo she said that was someone she knew as Marie Johnson. She also said that she was a mad chaser after males. Anna – or Marie – hadn't been working in our hotel, so she gave me the name of a chambermaid in the same place where Anna had worked, and I organised to meet with her. She was rather cagey about everything, but she said I should go and speak to Vic who's assistant manager at the Screwball disco at Hermit Park, so I went there this morning.

'Vic was female despite the name, and she was quite upset when she heard that Anna'd been murdered. She also knew her as Marie Johnson, and she also said that Anna tended to throw herself at guys. She didn't want to single any one male out at first, but then she said the son of the Townsville mayor was one who was a regular there, and that he was worse than most. She said that amongst other things she thought he might be dealing in drugs. It was all a bit vague, but I thought I should pass on those comments to you in case they're of any help. I should also add that she didn't want her name linked publicly with any of that information, so if there's a chance to keep the source quiet that'd be good.'

'Thanks, Nicholas – that's actually all very interesting. We haven't been making a lot of progress yet. We'd picked up that she was using an assumed name, and also that she'd left Townsville about ten days before the probable date of her murder. As far as we can find out she went up north, but we can't find out exactly where.'

'Well, I don't know if it'd be any help but Vic mentioned that the mayor of Townsville has various properties around the place, including one at somewhere called Iron Range which she said was well up the Cape York Peninsula.'

'Hm, that's certainly up north if anywhere is. Maybe we should pay a visit up there and see if anyone remembers her. She was a fairly distinctive character by the sound of it – the sort that you'd notice around. Let me think about this for a few hours, and maybe discuss it with one bloke in the station here who's a reasonable guy, and then I'll get back to you.'

* * *

I didn't hear anything for the rest of that day, but next morning Alan Campbell was in the hotel bright and early, looking excited, while I was still finishing breakfast.

He came and sat with me in the dining room and said: 'I

think we're making some progress. I'm not going to say anything in public here, but maybe we could go up to your room after and I'll tell you then.'

'Sure. Sounds good. Would you like a cup of coffee in the meantime?'

'Just had one, thanks.' He sounded keen not to delay further.

Back in the room he said: 'I spoke with my mate at the station and mentioned the possible drug angle, and he said this is a very live issue at the moment, but it's not the Queensland Police taking the lead on it, it's the Feds. The Australian Federal Police, that is. They take on crimes that go beyond the borders of a single state, particularly where there's a national interest involved. We'll have to be a bit careful here because there's often a degree of friction between federal and state on this sort of thing. However, we've got a legitimate case to follow up – a murder that took place in our state – and nobody can stop that.

'It seems the Feds think that regular shipments of drugs are coming in via somewhere up the Cape York Peninsula, but they haven't managed to pin it down yet. There's a big port for aluminium at Weipa, which is fairly well controlled but the people there aren't necessarily looking for drugs. There's also a small wharf near Iron Range, at Cape Weymouth which is near something called Portland Roads. There's a remote holiday resort there – could be somewhere where drugs could get in. And there's several other landing places around, and they can't all be watched thoroughly.

'The Feds haven't managed to get direct visual evidence of incoming material, and they haven't managed to intercept any in transit southwards. At the moment they're apparently trying to work out a way they can set up some remote surveillance but they can't quite decide which spots or spots to concentrate on. It's work still in progress.

'I've been trying to work out how to handle this, and my gut feeling is that I should go to the head Fed and tell him about our angle, and try to negotiate a way that we can both do our jobs without interfering with the other. And if we're really lucky we might get some synergy between the two. My mate says the Fed's a reasonable sort of guy, so it might work.

'Apparently what they're particularly worried about is tipping off the people doing the shipments. They'd simply shut down for a while, or find somewhere else, and they absolutely don't want that. So the Feds aren't going to be keen on us barging in there and asking lots of questions, and we'd need to have some sort of cover that wouldn't arouse anyone's suspicions. That's where I thought you might be able to come in.'

He looked at me. I was probably looking a bit bemused and worried, but he said: 'If you're feeling well enough to travel again, and if you don't need to get back to Flyblown Downs or whatever they call it to keep going on with your research, I was wondering whether you and I could become a small biological survey expedition up to Iron Range? After what you've just told me I'd like to find out exactly where Anna was hanging around and seen last – that might narrow the areas of interest down quite a bit.'

I thought for a moment. The doctor's tablets that I'd been taking certainly seemed to be helping me. 'Well, I'm pretty sure I'm well enough to travel again, and the research back at Flyblown isn't very important – mine was a bit mickey mouse anyway. Marion's was the real stuff. But what sort of biological survey did you have in mind? We'd have to be convincing or we'd stand out.'

'My first thought was that we could be looking for signs of bird diseases in the area of the wharf. You're a bird expert, aren't you? Even if you're not a hundred percent up on the disease side, you'd know more than any of the locals up there. Anything to do with quarantine in northern Australia's very plausible – there's endless surveys on that these days.'

'Okay, you're on if you want to. I'd have to get a message back to Marion somehow, though we needn't spell out the detail in case it gets intercepted – we can just say that I'm better but I'm not coming back for a bit longer. And what about logistics? I don't know the area at all, but I imagine it doesn't have hotels or motels or anything?'

'No, we'd have to look after ourselves, both sleeping and feeding. But don't you worry about that – I'm sure I can dig up enough suitable equipment from here for us. The police up here often have to go bush, and they'd have suitable gear available. I'll go and see what I can muster, and I'll be back later.'

He came back that afternoon and said: 'I've got us a four wheel drive vehicle, and one two-man tent. We'll have to share, but I'm told that I don't snore. There's also some cooking gear, but no food yet. However, there's a few places up the Peninsula where you can get a feed. For sleeping they don't run to folding beds here, but I've got us a pair of thick swags that'll be plenty comfortable. Would you be okay to leave tomorrow morning?'

'I would, but you'd better tell me a bit about the area before we go.'

'Right, I'll go and get a map.'

He came back in a few minutes and spread a large and detailed map of far north Queensland on the bed.

'Okay, we're here in Townsville. Up the coast you go through sugar cane areas and on to Cairns, which is a major tourist centre. After that the population gets pretty thin on the ground.

'This pointy bit up the top of Queensland's the Cape York Peninsula. The aluminium mining that I mentioned is here at Weipa' – he pointed on the map – 'and there's a lot of aboriginal communities and missions in various parts. Just off the northern tip is Thursday Island, which is a central spot for activities around that area. Much of the population that far up is Torres Strait Islander rather than aboriginal.

'The western side of the peninsula's relatively dry – open scrub forest – but on the eastern side there are some significant patches of rainforest, with varying degrees of protection. They're the sort of places that are always getting surveys of one sort or another. You may have heard of the Daintree rainforest, which is around here, and further north is Iron Range which also has some good rainforest. Iron Range also has a bit of interesting history because a small airfield was constructed there during the Second World War. A bloody isolated spot to be posted, I'd reckon. History buffs go up there to see it. I don't know whether or not small planes can still land there – if they can, that could be a way in for drugs.

'In terms of the economy of the area, after the aluminium ore I'd think that cattle'd be the next biggest earners – maybe in total they'd be more than the mining, I don't know – and then there's tourism. People like to drive all the way up to the tip of the Cape just to say they've been there, and there's that eco-resort at Cape Weymouth that I mentioned. That's just here on the eastern edge of the Iron Range National Park. It means that there's a small but steady flow of tourists through the area who could be smuggling drugs, except in the wet season when many of the roads are impassable.'

I thought for a few moments. 'I guess there'd be no harm in having an initial look-see up there – I could probably sound convincing enough for a survey. I can't quite think what we might find, but you never know until you get there, do you?'

'Good man. I'll go and get some gear together, and we can start in the morning.'

MARION

Life had become a bit quiet at Flyblown Downs, with Nicholas away sick in Townsville and Gil Reynolds in Melbourne. There was nothing wrong with Frank Feeney and Mike Tandouris, but they had no real interest in any flying object that was larger than a small biting fly, and I missed being able to discuss the results of my survey with Nicholas. I'd gathered quite a lot of background information on the general ecology of Australian crows and some of the birds of prey, though not so much to do with damage to Australian livestock. If there was any.

The camp became busier again when Gil returned from Melbourne, though it didn't become much cheerier because he was annoyed by his failure to locate the fly larvae that he wanted, and he was spitting chips about his reception by Anna Ioannides' father.

The next day over the evening meal he announced that he'd nearly finished collecting the full range of maggots available in that area. That rang some alarm bells with me.

'Does that mean you'll be packing up this camp and moving on, then?' I asked. I could see myself suddenly being left without a camp or backup.

'Well, we might be rid of Gil, but the workers of the world'll still be here,' said Frank. 'Me and Mike have to get a full year's data on the populations of biting flies in this region, so we've got a few months yet. Thank God for the bridge which stops life being totally boring, though Gil'll stuff that up if he moves on.'

'You could start reading, if you can still remember how to do that,' Gil said. 'And that reminds me, I've brought back something for Marion to read – an airline magazine from my flight down to Melbourne. It's got an article in it on a bird of paradise that's native to Australia, and I thought you being a bird person might find it interesting. The bird's called Victoria's riflebird, and it's got some remarkable habits like all the birds of paradise.'

I said: 'Gee, that does surprise me. If you'd asked me I'd have said that there aren't any birds of paradise in Australia. I thought they're only found in Papua New Guinea?'

'Well, the great majority are, but according to the article there are four species in Australia. They all live in forested areas, two of them only in the far north of the Cape York Peninsula and two further south – in fact one of them comes south almost to Sydney. They aren't nearly as spectacular as the ones in PNG, but if you read the article and look at the pictures of the male dancing, you'll see that they're still pretty remarkable.'

Gil went and got the magazine, and I looked at the pictures, which showed both male and female birds. The female was a fairly ordinary bird, with a dark brown back and a prettily speckled pale brown breast. It had a thin, down-curved bill with a touch of yellow behind it, and a narrow white flash over the eye. The male, on the other hand, was basically jet black and glossy, with a bluish tinge on the top of the head, a flash of shining blue under the chin, and a grey-green area on the breast. Most remarkable, however, was when it took up its courtship pose. It curled its wings out and up on either side, coming forward in two crescents that almost encircled the bird's body, and it threw its head back and opened its bill.

'That's beautiful. Quite extraordinary,' I said. 'I'd love to read the whole article, if you don't mind me hanging on to it for a bit.'

'You're welcome to keep it. You're the bird expert, after all. And you can take it back to the UK and show other bird people that we aren't only a continent of screeching cockatoos.'

That evening, when we were sitting down after eating and washing up, I said to Gil: 'Do you have to be a necrophile or whatever they're called to enjoy fishing around in carcasses for maggots?'

'Well, I wouldn't quite say "enjoy" is the right word, but you do get used to it. And the more I see of maggots the more I think they're actually interesting creatures.'

'In any ways that I'd understand?'

'Well, for a start, they're nature's cleaner-uppers. Most of them are totally harmless, and they get into all sorts of dead and decaying organic matter that would just lie around if it weren't for maggots to recycle them. And not many organisms could survive and prosper in the conditions under which they live. As I was saying to Alan the other day, they're very neat the way they shut down as they go into anything gooey, and then how their spiracles immediately clear when they come back out. But when you look across all the different families of flies, there's a huge variety of maggot habits many of which are pretty smart. Some are parasites of other insects or other organisms, some are predators, some live in marine environments, one can live in hot water springs at temperatures up to 50 degrees C. One even lives in pools of crude oil where it seeps up through the soil. For a long time entomologists thought that they must feed on the crude oil, which would be a pretty remarkable diet for an insect. Then someone spoiled that myth by finding that they were actually eating insects that fell on to the surface of the oil and got trapped there.'

'Some of them are pretty nasty though, aren't they? Like that screwworm you were talking about.'

'Yes, but they're a small minority. There are two screw-worms, an Old World species and a New World one, and they both attack live cattle. There are also a few that are parasites of humans where they live in boils under the skin, or of animals where they live in the nasal cavity. But most flies of those families wait for their meat to be dead, so they're still clearers-up. Actually the one I like best is a species of blowfly that feeds in human wounds, but all it eats is the bacteria in the wound. Those ones are used in medicine in some places, because they're the most effective and safe way to clean up nasty wounds. I believe they even secrete an antibiotic to help clean the wound. You just have to get a patient who doesn't mind the thought of it.'

I didn't get round to reading Gil's article on the birds of paradise for a couple of days, and when I did I found that it covered more than just birds of paradise. It covered various elements of the fauna that were mostly known from Papua New Guinea but did occur in Australia as well, and among them were two tree kangaroos. I'd never even heard of kangaroos that lived in trees, so I asked Gil about them over the evening meal.

'It does ring a very faint bell,' he said, 'but I can't give you any detail.'

At that point Frank Feeney piped up. 'I do know a bit about them, actually. I did an assignment on them when I was doing my honours degree. If I remember right there are two different species in Oz. I know one's called Lumholtz's tree kangaroo and it's found on the Atherton Tableland, same as one of the birds of paradise. I think the other's called Bennett's tree kangaroo, and it's found from the Daintree River north. That's further north than Atherton.'

I said: 'Well, a thought crossed my mind when I read all that. If both birds and kangaroos can span the gap between Papua New Guinea and Australia, why not some insects as well? Such as blowflies…? Ones with curly spiracles like in your specimens…?'

There was a long silence, while Gil stared into the distance. Finally he said: 'You might just have a point there. We've collected on the Atherton Tableland and it wasn't there. We've also collected up to about Mossman, but the critical rainforests could be the ones north of there. Two of the birds of paradise only occur in the very far northern rainforests, and one of the tree kangaroos. As I said the other day, I've nearly done as much as I can in this area – I wouldn't mind maybe going right up the Cape York Peninsula and surveying there. I might get in touch with Alan Campbell and let him know what we've just been talking about. I reckon he'll be a lot happier if his body came from north Queensland than PNG, even if it was the far north. I'll get in touch with him first thing tomorrow.'

Next morning there was a long satellite phone call, and Gil then came back to report.

'Alan's pretty keen on the idea, and he wants an immediate survey if it's possible. I think he's under a bit of pressure to make some progress with that case, but he filled me in on the progress that they have so far made. By the way, Marion, he said that Nicholas is a fair bit better now. Part of the progress with the case has also been due to Nicholas. Apparently the chambermaid in the hotel where he was recuperating knew Anna Ioannides, though under a different name, and Nicholas got a contact who might have known what actually happened to her. She didn't unfortunately, but she did provide several useful bits of information, which also point to the Cape York Peninsula. So I told him about your idea, Marion, and Alan's really pricked up his ears. He's now keener than ever to get a quick survey of maggots up the Peninsula. He told me that he and Nicholas were planning to go up there anyway, with Nicholas as cover for the investigations they're planning to undertake. I think he must have put the hard word on Nicholas. They'd cooked up some cock and bull story about a survey of bird diseases that Nicholas was going to be leading.'

I'm afraid I snorted when I heard that. 'That would be the blind leading the blind. I reckon that Alan would know as much about bird diseases as Nicholas does. It would probably be along the lines of: "If it looks wobbly it's probably sick. If it drops down dead then it definitely was sick".'

Gil grinned. 'That explains why Alan was so keen when I offered him a real survey, and I think I've also given him hope for a more sensible solution than PNG. Marion, if you're okay to stay here and keep your work going, I'll go to Townsville as soon as I can and the three of us can go north. But if you'd like to come with us I'm sure that'd be fine by Alan too.'

I probably looked rather wistful because I'd have loved to see the Cape York area, but I did owe it to the government conservation body which was funding me to get some results for them. Perhaps there'd be a chance to still get up there with Nicholas when my project was finished. I said: 'I think I'd better stay here. I do need to get some results to justify my grant, and anyway too large an expedition might look suspicious.'

ALAN CAMPBELL

Nicholas and I were all packed and ready to go north when Gil Reynolds arrived from the bush. Luckily he'd brought his own camping equipment and four-wheel drive, so we were able to head almost straight off. I'd planned out a strategy which I floated past Gil, and we agreed on the first step which was that he as a scientist would take the running in any questions or negotiations, and I'd simply look like a hanger-on. After that we'd decide how to play it depending on how things were going.

I'd been doing some background on Mal Robertson, the mayor of Townsville, who'd been the person named as having a number of cattle properties in far north Queensland, including the Cape York peninsula. When I checked it out I found they were quite extensive, and I decided the first step should be to call on the mayor "as a courtesy" to seek his advice on the survey. It'd be interesting to see whether he became at all defensive about having people poking around on his properties.

We discovered that there was little council business currently on, so the mayor was not in Townsville – he was at his home at Mount Spec, about seventy kilometres north of

Townsville. It was up the Bruce Highway and then inland a bit into an area of rainforest. I decided we shouldn't forewarn the mayor – just say that we'd been passing and we'd decided to call in on the spur of the moment.

We left the highway, and the road gradually climbed up the Paluma Range. From Crystal Creek onwards there was some fine rainforest, and it was even finer where the house stood, in a clearing completely ringed by lush trees hung with vines. The house itself was a classic old Queenslander – an extensive single floor entirely surrounded by a wide verandah, standing up on high timber supports and in very good condition.

We climbed up to the main verandah and called out: 'Anyone home?'

We could hear scuffling inside, and after a moment a middle-aged woman appeared in the doorway, accompanied by a very small, pointy-faced dog. The woman was dressed like a Brisbane matron of about thirty years ago ready for a morning tea reception – not at all the sort of gear you'd expect to see out in the bush.

'Can I help you?' she enquired a bit uncertainly. The pointy-faced dog bared its teeth at us.

As agreed, Gil did the talking. 'Would you be Mrs Robertson by any chance?'

'Yes, I am.' She looked even more doubtful.

'My name's Gil Reynolds and I work for the Department of Primary Industry. We're doing a survey of agricultural pests up the Cape York Peninsula, and as your family are large landholders in the area we thought we'd call in as a matter of courtesy to let you know. Would your husband be here at the moment?'

'I'm afraid he's just gone down to the paddock for a moment.' She sounded a bit flustered. 'Maybe you'd like to come in and wait – he shouldn't be too long.'

We went into what was obviously a formal reception room. Incongruously for a room in the tropical bush, it had pastel-coloured wool carpeting all over the floor. She sat us down and offered tea and coffee, which we happily accepted.

While she was out we could hear a continual low snarling sound, which we realised was coming from under a vacant chair. A face became associated with it, and it was the pointy-faced micro-dog that had been at the front door. It had obviously snuck into the room with us.

Mrs Robertson came back with a tray with drinks and biscuits, and sat down with us. The dog then advanced towards us, baring its teeth further and growling. Finally it made a sudden dart at Gil, who was wearing sandals, and bit his large toe.

Gil exclaimed sharply and pulled his foot back.

'Naughty Bandy!' said Mrs Robertson fondly. 'Come back here to Mummy.'

The dog retreated reluctantly to her chair, from where it continued to make aggressive noises.

'I'm sorry but he just gets a little wary of strangers. He's a pedigree dog and he's very highly strung.'

Little bastard, more like, I thought, but I couldn't really say anything. We did want to meet the mayor.

'He's a pedigree miniature Doberman. His name's Champion Bandecourt Farquhar the third, but we call him Bandy for short. He's really a little darling.'

Gil was wriggling his foot, and he dabbed at it with a tissue.

At that moment a large, overbearing man strode into the room. At his entry Mrs Robertson visibly shrank, and seemed to be cowering away from her husband a bit. He said rather aggressively to her: 'Who are these people?' He made no greeting to us.

'They're scientists, darling, from the Department of Primary Industry. They want to do a survey on our properties.'

Christ, I thought. Not quite the intro that Gil wanted.

'Good morning, Mr Robertson. My name's Gil Reynolds and I work for QDPI. I was just telling your wife that we're about to survey insects of quarantine significance, particularly exotic blowflies that might threaten cattle, up the Cape York Peninsula. It hasn't ever been surveyed fully to date. We were passing on our way north, and as we'd heard that you're one of the most important landowners up that way' – he was bunging it on pretty well – 'we thought we'd let you know about this. We'll probably be asking to go on to one or two of your properties to take samples of livestock flies. One of the things we'll be most watching for is screwworm which is only just over the water in PNG. As I'm sure you know it can cause a lot of damage to cattle when it just eats into a live beast and causes a wound that can get infected.'

Robertson said nothing but looked at his wife again. 'What have you told them?'

'Absolutely nothing, dear. I just made them a cup of tea while we waited for you. I think I'll just go and check my baking in the kitchen.'

'Right. You'd better take Bandecourt with you as well.'

'Come on Bandy – you can come and help Mummy in the kitchen. Cakies!'

The dog backed slowly out into the hallway, growling all the while.

Bloody hell, I thought. What sort of a place have we come into?

Robertson turned and looked at us for the first time. 'Right, well, thanks for letting me know about your survey. What sort of access would you be looking for on my properties?'

My properties, not ours, I noted. A charming character all round.

'We'd contact the manager first, of course. We'd ask to come on to the property in an area where there are some cattle not too far away, and put out some traps baited with meat that's just beginning to go off. There's no danger to human or bovine health – the material's all in enclosed containers. We expose them for several days, and then take them away and process them to see what's laid its eggs into the baits. We'd also collect any flies that are buzzing around the traps, using simple insect nets. And that's all there is to it.'

'Right, well, I suppose that's okay then. I'll get you a list of the properties, their managers and their contact details. I'd be grateful if you could keep any disturbance of the property sites to a minimum.'

'Of course,' said Gil. He wouldn't of course have any real intention of following that instruction.

As Robertson left the room we just looked at each other, and a few eyebrows were raised.

Robertson was back in a few minutes. 'Here's the list – it should be straightforward. Now if you'll excuse me I've got some urgent business to attend to.'

'Thank you,' said Gil. 'And please thank Mrs Robertson for the tea.'

'Hmph,' said Robertson, who didn't seem inclined to do any such thing.

We left the house and went back to the vehicles. As we got to where we were parked I said: 'Jesus, what a charming piece of work. I hope he's up to his eyeballs in illegal activities, and we can throw the book at him. I suspect there's something, certainly, the way he wanted to know what his wife had said to us, and he's certainly not keen on having us poking around.'

'Yeah,' said Gil. 'And I hope we can incriminate little Bandicoot Fuckwit as well.'

'How's the toe, mate. Did it do much damage?'

'It's not too bad, but it did bleed a bit. What a shame that some of the blood went on the pastel carpet, too....'

* * *

We returned to the main highway and drove north through extensive areas of sugar cane to the town of Tully, where we stopped for lunch at La Bella Vista café in the main street. The *bella vista* from the café turned out to be of buildings in the main street, that were blackened with mould from the very humid climate. I recalled that Tully's supposed to have the highest annual rainfall of any town in Australia. Inside the Bella Vista there seemed to be as much Italian as Australian being spoken. A lot of the cane farmers up that way were of Italian descent, and they were obviously keeping their language very much alive.

Over lunch I pulled out a map of the Cape York Peninsula, and we looked at the list of properties in relation to the map.

'Right, we're looking at these from two points of view. One is whether or not it's near the sea and some sort of landing place, in relation to possible importation of drugs. The second is whether or not there might have been some involvement in the murder of Anna Ioannides. I don't quite know how we can assess that, though. Maybe we could talk to locals and see if they remember a feisty Greek girl up there with a male.

'Robertson's got five different properties, which is a bit more than I was expecting. This one near Mount Carbine's pretty small, and it's nowhere near the sea. This one up near Iron Range is a definite possibility. It must be either in rainforest or close to some, and it's also near a landing area at Cape Weymouth. We certainly need to go up there, and Gil needs to trap comprehensively around there.

'There's also one over here near Weipa, just past Merluna Station, which I hadn't expected. It won't be rainforest round there, but it's not that far from Weipa which I think I told you, Nicholas, is a large port for export of bauxite. Plenty of coming and going there, and not easy to monitor it all.

'Then there's this one between Dunbar and Rutland Plains. That's definitely dry woodland or even more open than that, but I think it's reasonably near to Ironbark Creek where Anna's body was found, which certainly makes it interesting from one perspective. Ironbark Creek's not on this map – I expect the mapmaker knew the place and decided it wasn't worth a mention – but I think it's about here.' I pointed to a spot near Vanrook Station.

'The final one's over here in the east, near Kalpowar Station.

No landing possibilities, and I don't think there's rainforest around there but I don't know the area well. It's probably one of the lower probabilities on our list.'

Lunch over, we headed on up the main highway to Cairns, and beyond towards Mossman. Just short of Mossman we turned inland towards Mount Molloy, and then onwards up the road that led into the Cape York Peninsula. At Mount Carbine we stopped, and I said: 'This is one of the places where Robertson has a property. I think we should make an early camp here – there's a campground just at the edge of the settlement, and we should have time to poke around a bit and start chatting to some locals. We can get a meal and a beer at the pub later.'

The campground looked fairly empty as we pulled in. This turned out to be a plus, because the man who ran the campground was obviously dying for a chat with someone, and he'd lived in the area for twenty-five years. We set up our tents and went back to the office.

'You'd probably know Mal Robertson, wouldn't you? I believe he's got a property only just outside the town.'

'Yeah, he's a short way up the road to Laura. There's a track going left a few k's out of town, and you go towards the St George River. Crystal Park, the property's called, though there isn't much crystal about it. Dry as arseholes, it is. You know Mal, do you?'

'Well, we've only met him the once, but we're doing a survey of pests of cattle in this area and north, and Mal's got several properties in the area. We thought we might drop in and ask if they get much problem with things attacking their cattle.'

'Well, good luck there then. The manager keeps himself

very much to himself, and they don't seem all that keen on outsiders going in. I've been trying to set up fishing expeditions for visitors to this area, to make a bit of extra cash for meself. I'd wanted to go through his property to get to the St George River, which is outside his land, but no deal. Bugger flatly refused.'

'D'you know Mal's son Wayne?'

'Yeah, more's the pity. He's in here every so often when he's on his way to one of the properties. He's thinks he's God's gift to the human race – especially the female half of it.'

'That's interesting, because a girl who my wife knows was coming up this way recently with him, and I was hoping to catch up with her while we're up this way. If we can find her, that is…'

He tailed off to invite a reply, and was rewarded.

'Well, a month or two ago he was through here with a sheila. Nice looker she was too, and pretty feisty with it. I reckon she might have been his match if anyone was.'

'D'you think she might still be up there?'

'No idea, mate. All I can say is she wasn't with him when he came back through some days later.'

'What would the manager's name be?'

'Buggered if I can tell you exactly. Some long and unpronounceable name it is – Polish, I think. He just calls himself Rad.'

'Well, we might just go and call on Rad to ask him about pests.'

'Mate, you won't be doing it at the moment. He left yesterday going south with some cattle they was shipping out. You might find one of the stockmen there, but I doubt he'd know much.'

We went back to our tents and discussed the news.

'I don't think there's much future in doing anything here after what we've heard,' I said. 'This property never fitted our criteria all that well. However, as we're here and we've got a bit of time left today, I wouldn't mind having a quick shufti at the property just to see what's there.'

We set off up the highway and found the left turn easily – there was a smart sign saying Crystal Park. A few k's down the track we got to a gate. A sign said in large letters "PRIVATE PROPERTY. ACCESS TO OK MINE ONLY. DO NOT LEAVE VEHICLE WHILE ON THIS LAND. NO SHOOTING."

We opened the gate and drove through, and on down the track until we saw some cattleyards and what must have been a homestead just past them. We drove up to the house and parked. The house was a high-blocked Queenslander, with a verandah round all four sides at the upper level. There was no vehicle at the house, and all seemed very quiet. We went up the steps to the front door and knocked. No response. We called out – still no response. We tried the door – locked. We walked round the whole of the verandah, but the place was firmly shut.

'Bugger,' I said. 'I'd have liked to have had at least a brief word with someone just to see what sort of people they are. Though I think we're beginning to get an idea of that anyway.'

'It's pretty dry country,' observed Gil. 'You wouldn't be getting any rainforest insects around here.'

'Yeah, I think we may as well cut our losses and move straight on tomorrow. But we can chat to a few people in the pub tonight about the property and Wayne. And Mal, maybe. There should be others around who'll know them.'

When we got there the pub wasn't all that busy. I went up to the barman.

'G'day, mate. Three schooners of Fourex, thanks.' The barman poured them.

'You'll have one yourself, mate?'

'Thanks but I'll put it on the slate if you don't mind. Much appreciated, though.'

I launched into the spiel about the survey, and then said: 'We'd been hoping to get a bit of cooperation from Mal Robertson's properties, like Crystal Park, but people around here don't seem to think they're all that public-spirited?'

'They'd be right there. I haven't got much time for 'em, for sure. Can't stand Mal Robertson. He's right up himself – a long way up. My brother's got a property near theirs, and he's been losing quite a few cattle over recent years. They're not getting through fences that are down – somebody's helping them on their way. And there's more than one in this area who thinks that's to do with the bloody Robertsons.'

'Jeez, that's not good, for sure. We actually went to the Crystal Park homestead but there wasn't anybody home. We had another reason for wanting to see them too – a young lass that my mother knows came up this way some weeks ago with Wayne Robertson, and we were hoping to catch up with her if she's still up this way.'

'God help her if she was with that mongrel. He's a nasty piece of work. He's a bludger. Dishonest. Violent with it at times. There's more than once that I've had to throw him out of this pub when he's picked a fight with someone.'

'Yeah, you're not the first person who's said that to us. Sounds charming.'

We ordered their meals from the bar – steak and chips seemed to be the only option. When they came the steaks were tough and overcooked, though the chips weren't too bad.

Gil said to Nicholas: 'I'm afraid this is a fairly typical introduction to the gourmet cooking of the north. All the good meat gets sent south, and the people up here get what's left. Even so, a good cook can do a bit better than this. Makes me appreciate young Tandouris at our place all the more. Don't tell him that, though – he's cheeky enough as it is.'

* * *

We struck camp early next day and continued north, through the small town of Laura and on to the slightly larger town of Coen. That was a drive of a bit over four hundred kilometres, along unsealed, sandy roads through relatively dry forest. It doesn't sound all that far, but the driving was fairly slow and it took us the best part of the day. We'd hoped to get further, but Coen had a good campground and a store selling provisions, so we decided to camp there for the night.

We went to the pub in the evening and once more asked about the Robertson properties – there was one a bit further up the road towards Iron Range. The publican said: 'You got a good reason for going there?'

'We're doing a survey of insects associated with livestock up this way. We heard that he's got a largeish property near Iron Range, and we wanted to do some sampling in that sort of country. Why were you asking?'

'Oh, it's just that they don't welcome outsiders. And they're bastards so I was hoping that maybe you were the law after them instead.'

That was a bit too close to the truth for comfort. 'No, it's a Primary Industries survey – we've just been doing the Gulf Country and now we're doing Cape York. But you reckon they won't be too keen on us there?'

'Well, the manager's a bit surly but you might be able to sweet talk him, but if Mal Robertson's up there I don't reckon you'll get anywhere. Bastard's one of those who thinks his shit doesn't stink. If you want to get some cooperation near Iron Range, me brother Ray's got a property right next to Robertson's – Pascoe Downs. He'd be quite interested in anything you're doing.'

'Thanks for all of that – always good to get the drum from someone local. We might call in on your brother too. Do you know if he's there at the moment?'

'I'm sure he is. He'll be getting ready to muster, but he'll be interested enough in what you're doing to spare an hour or two. I'll be calling him a bit later on tonight. Do you want me to tell him you might be dropping in?'

'That'd be great, thanks. How far up the road is he?'

'It's about forty k's or so – probably close to an hour's driving. The last bit off the main road's a bit slow.'

'Would you like to tell him that we'll be there around half past ten, eleven? And is it easy to find?'

'Yeah, there's a good new signpost at the junction with the highway, and signs after that as well. He's only about fifteen k's from the main road.'

'Great. I'll look forward to meeting Ray. Now, we'll have three schooners of whatever you think's your best beer, and have one yourself while you're at it.'

'Thanks, mate – coming right up.'

We took our beers to one of the tables, and I said: 'You

might wonder why I agreed that we might go to Pascoe Downs, but it's because I thought that we might get some almost first-hand info about Robertson's property from someone who's an immediate neighbour, and if we're really lucky he might have seen Anna Ioannides if she was actually in the area.'

'You reckon we can con him enough about our survey to carry it off?' asked Gil.

'What do you mean, you're supposed to be the expert on all this! Of course you can. After all you are going to sample insects even if it's only to chase down this PNG fly, and if you did happen to come across some other nasties, well, it's all useful information for pest control.'

We drank for a moment, and then Gil said: 'Mal Robertson doesn't seem to be up there in the local popularity stakes, does he?'

Nicholas said: 'After his behaviour when we were at his place and he walked in, I can understand why. I thought that was bloody rude, myself.'

'Too right, mate, and that sort of thing doesn't go down well with the average Aussie, especially up here. With a bit of luck the general animosity might help us to hear things that wouldn't otherwise be said. That's why I'm quite keen to go to Pascoe Downs.'

We drank to that.

* * *

We found the turnoff to Pascoe Downs easily, as the pub owner had said. He was also right about the access road – it was pretty rough. However, when we reached the homestead we got a warm welcome, and the billy was on the fire just outside.

'G'day, I'm Ray. Me brother Stuey told me youse'd be up here this morning. Have a seat and I'll get you some tea.'

'G'day, I'm Gil and I'm leading this survey. That's Alan with the mo, and this here's Nicholas. Tea'd be great – thanks, mate.'

Tea was poured. It didn't hit the cups with a clang, but it seemed close to solid tannin when we drank it.

Ray said: 'You're after screwworms and the like. I saw them buggers in PNG one time, and they're real nasty. They leave a big raw hole in the side of a beast, and then you can get infections and God knows what in the wound.'

'Too right, I've seen 'em too and we certainly don't want 'em in here.'

Then he gave us a long stare. 'But I reckon you might be after something else as well. You're cops, aintcha?'

That took me back a bit. 'What makes you think that?' was all I could think to say.

'Your wagon over there. The number plate's PRS 567. That wagon's been here before, and last time it came it was being driven by two cops from the stock squad in Townsville. They came here when I reported some of me beasts missing.'

'You sure it was the same number? It could have been similar.'

'Nah, I'm sure. PRS is my initials – Peter Raymond Smith, and I remember that the 567 ran rather nicely. I was thinking I wouldn't have minded them plates on my own wagon. And I reckon you look like a cop, too. Not so sure about the other two.'

He said all this in a neutral tone – not hostile, but not particularly friendly either. Just our bloody luck about that number plate. I had to do some quick thinking.

'Mate, you're half right and half wrong. We are indeed up here to do a survey of fly maggots of quarantine importance. Gil here's been doing that in the Gulf Country for some months, and he's now shifting to the Far North of the Peninsula. Pretty relevant because it's so near to PNG. Nicholas here's also an expert biologist, but you're right that I'm a cop.

'However, my mission up here's also related to maggots. I'm looking for evidence relating to a murder victim. She was found in the Gulf Country, but all the signs are that she was killed in rainforest, possibly somewhere up this way, and after a few days the body was carted away to the Gulf Country and buried there. There were a lot of maggots in the body, and they were of a type that's never found in the dry Gulf country. It's probably found up here, and that's what I'm here to confirm. I'm normally based in Brisbane, and the only wagon I could get quickly was this one from the Townsville police. Well spotted, by the way. I wish all of our guys were as observant as that.'

I didn't think that was giving anything away that mattered, and I hoped it would pacify him. It did.

'Jeez, that's a bit of a tale all right. If there's anything I can do to help either of your missions just let me know.'

'Well, you have the advantage that you're a local and you know the area and the people better than most. The body that was found was a young woman, and she was killed a couple of months ago or a bit less. Her identity's known, and from what we've heard she was a fairly lively and feisty lass – the sort who'd be noticed when she came to a new area, especially one like this where you probably don't get all that many feisty young women coming in. Does that ring any bells with anyone you saw?'

'Well, you're right about not many young women coming this way. A few naturalists, that's about all. But there was one I remember, and the timing might just fit in with what you said. You came down our access road off the highway, but it doesn't only service our property – it goes on past our gate to Forestview station. They're the mob that we reckon have been stealing our cattle. Anyway, about a couple of months or so ago – coulda been a bit less or more – I was coming back home and a four-wheel drive was broken down on the track just before our gate. I stopped to help, and found that all that had happened was the distributor cap had come loose so the engine wasn't firing. Stupid bastard who was driving should have spotted that. If you drive in country like this you need to know a little bit about vehicles.'

'Did you recognise the couple?'

'The driver I did. It was the son of the guy who owns Forestview. The owner's Mal Robertson from near Townsville, and his son's Wayne. A right prick and a nasty piece of work. The sheila I didn't know, but she seemed quite a lively sort like you were saying.'

'Can you describe her?'

'Well, she was a bit taller than the average sheila, and she stood pretty straight. She had a longish neck, and a long, thin face. Not pretty but very striking, and I'd say she had a pretty lively character. She should have been able to do better than that arsehole Wayne.'

'That actually sounds quite like the person we're following up on. I don't suppose you saw her again after that time.'

'Nah, I didn't, but I wouldn't normally expect to. I don't go on to their property if I can help it. They don't welcome any sort of outsiders, even neighbours. If I need to ask about missing stock, me mate the cop from Coen goes and does that for me.'

'And as far as you know she's no longer around this area?'

'Don't think so, but as I said I wouldn't really know.'

'Well, that's a very helpful lead to follow up. Thank you. Now to the other part of our mission – the maggot survey. Do you have any patches of thick scrub on the property? Thick jungly bits?'

'Yeah, we've got a few certainly. I could show you.'

'No need, if you could just point us in the direction. Gil, tell Ray what we'd like to do.'

Gil said: 'What we'd like to do is put out some baits of meat and let them go off for a few days, so that the various types of flies lay eggs in them and the eggs hatch to maggots. Then we pick them up again, take them back to the lab, collect the maggots and identify them. The meat's enclosed in cages, and there's no disease or other threat to your animals. And we wouldn't disturb any of the beasts either.'

'No problem. I'll get you a sketch map of the property and mark the patches of scrub, and you can go and look at them. I guess you guys are used to bush-bashing enough for that?'

'We should be, some of the places we've been to.'

Ray went in to get the map, and we had a quick confab.

'I was a bit thrown when he spotted that I was a cop, but I think in the end it's worked out quite a plus – that thing about Wayne Robertson having a female who could just have been Anna is very interesting. He was already a person of interest after what you heard in Townsville, Nicholas, and I reckon he is even more now.

'I was thinking on my feet when I said that we might set some traps on this property – I hope that's okay with you both. Gil, you could get an overall collection for your study, and I could check whether this PNG fly's here, if it's the right sort of vegetation type. That okay with you?'

'Sounds good to me,' said Gil. 'We could do a recce once we get the map and pick the best areas, and then we can go away and prepare some traps. It sounds as though Ray won't mind if we come and go a bit here.'

Ray returned with the sketch plan and marked in the best areas of rainforest. We had a quick look at it, and I thought to ask: 'Any particular risks in the jungle up here?'

'Yeah, there's a few, but nothing you shouldn't be able to cope with. There's some large carpet snakes, and a few smaller ones, but they generally hear you before you see them and they head off the other way. There's plenty of leeches, but if you've got good footwear and no exposed bits of leg, no problem. Watch out as well for the lawyer vines – they can give you slashes across the face with their spines, as well as catching on your gear. You might also see the odd cassowary, and if you startle them they can give you quite a nasty jab. Best to avoid them if you see them. There's no free water in the area so you'd be unlucky to come across any crocs. I guess the biggest danger's wild pigs. There's quite a few of them in this area, and some of 'em are huge. They're real aggressive if you meet one. Get the hell out of it then – quick as you can.'

I looked at the others. 'The gouge marks on Miss Ioannides' body. I've seen the pictures, and I reckon they could have been signs of eating by pigs. They'd go for dead meat, wouldn't they, mate?'

'Too right they would. They rip into anything they find that's dead, and they don't mess around. Nasty buggers, they are.'

'Well, I don't reckon there'd be any wild pigs much around Ironbark Creek – the country's too open there. So it's another thought that maybe she was exposed first in a forested area. I guess all the forests round this way would have wild pigs?'

'Too right they would. Bloody menace, they are.' I was getting the idea that Ray didn't like wild pigs at all.

'Just one more thought. We've been talking to you about an investigation that's still under way, and it's a bit sensitive. We wouldn't want anyone involved to hear in advance that we're looking around here, so I'd be grateful if you could keep this completely to yourself at the moment.'

'No worries, mate. I hope you catch the bastard that done it.'

'Okay then, we might go and have a recce of some of your patches of scrub if that's all right with you.'

'Go for it, guys, it's not going to worry anyone here. Just ask if you need anything more, or any information.' Then he added, grinning: 'No offence meant when I said you looked like a cop, mate. The cop in Coen's one of me good mates, though I won't repeat what he says about Brisbane cops.'

'No offence taken, either. And you might find that I share his views about some of my Brizzie colleagues....'

GIL REYNOLDS

We picked the four largest patches of rainforest shown on the map and went to look at each in turn. I figured that the larger they were the more likely they were to have undisturbed and complete faunas.

The first patch was just about impenetrable. We weren't going to have the time to hack our way in, and we couldn't really do that on someone else's land anyway.

The second patch was a bit more open but was still good varied jungle vegetation, with palms, vines, a few tree ferns and all the assorted trees and lesser plants that make up Australian rainforest. We wandered into it, and some way in we located an area where we could set traps and expect to get any of the fauna that was living there.

The third and fourth were pretty similar, and it looked as though I could do some very effective sampling there. I thought I would set traps in at least two of the areas – three if I could make up enough with the gear that I'd brought. It might also depend on the supply of meat available. We hadn't noticed any fresh roadkill on the way here, so it would depend on how much fresh meat the Coen butcher had available. The traps would need reasonably large pieces of bait so that they didn't dry out too fast and lose their attractiveness. Not all flies go to carrion immediately it starts to smell.

We decided to go back to the camp and start rigging up traps. We stopped off at the house to let Ray know that we'd be back, but he wasn't there. We did, however, meet his wife so we could leave a message with her. She was a cheery soul, who said that Ray did all the running of the property and she did all the domestic stuff, and anything outdoors that was okay with him was okay with her.

Alan and Nicholas offered to help put the traps together, so I had to show them what was involved.

'You've got to have traps that won't be interfered with too much by the local fauna. Various things walking past can knock traps over accidentally, but the greater threat is from animals that want to get at the meat inside the trap for food. Specially wild pigs, by the sound of it. So we pin the meat against the bottom floor so that even if the trap is knocked right over the meat doesn't fall out.

'The other hazard is insects, slugs, snails and whatever, crawling into the trap at ground level and stuffing up the baits or eating them altogether. We're only after things that fly in from above, so we put stages down at ground level and then set the traps on top, pinned to the bases again so that they can't fall over. And the whole set-up gets skewered on to the ground to hold it in place. It's not a hundred percent foolproof, but most of them should be all right.'

I showed the others what to do, and left them to it while I

went to negotiate with the Coen butcher for meat. There was probably going to be some judgement needed on what would be suitable as baits.

I went into the butcher's shop and explained what I was after and why. The butcher looked a bit bemused at first, but when I told him that the study would help protect the livestock of the area he got quite enthusiastic.

'Well, you're in luck, mate, because I got a fresh delivery of meat in this morning. We were getting a bit low until then. What exactly would you like?'

'Beef'd be best, but lamb, pork or chicken would also do, in that order. And the quality doesn't matter at all. It can be rough as guts and it's still fine, so anything at all that's meat'll do and I'll give you a fair price for it. Not that I'm suggesting that your meat isn't top quality, of course,' I added quickly, because he was looking at me slightly sideways. 'It's just that I know suppliers sometimes put some less good stuff in with the good, and you could move that on to me if there is any. The flies don't know any different.'

'Yeah, well, it can be a bit variable, you're right. I'll go and see what there is.'

He went out to the back, and came back with a selection of pieces of steak that were certainly close to the "rough as guts" level. As Alan had told Nicholas the other night, the good stuff gets sent south.

I picked out a number of pieces, more than the number of traps that I thought we'd be able to set up, and made the purchase. The butcher looked pretty pleased with the sale, and I thought that we were well in business. We should have enough time to get the traps in place and set today if the other two had assembled them right, so I headed back to the camp.

They hadn't done too bad a job for beginners, so we grabbed a quick bite of late lunch and headed back to Ray's. We did have enough traps to set them in the three good patches of forest. When the last was done I waited for a little while to watch what came to them. There were a few miscellaneous flies cruising round in the area, but no obvious blowflies. Not surprising really – the meat was still too fresh. It would need to hum a bit before it would be attractive.

We went back to the camp and discussed a timetable for the next few days. I said: 'We might go back tomorrow morning to check that the traps haven't been knocked around too much by wild animals, but after that I'll have to leave them out for about four days to make sure that all possible flies have laid in them. At these temperatures that should be enough time. So we'll have several spare days – you can decide, Alan, what might be the best way to spend them.'

'Hm. Since we're so close, maybe it would be an idea to have a look at Mal Robertson's place next door – Forestview or whatever it's called. Imaginative name, eh? We got Mal's clearance to go in as we needed – the manager can't be too obstructive in that case. Can he?'

We adjourned to the pub with a good feeling about today. One small step forward towards a result, with luck.

THE BRUCE HIGHWAY, CENTRAL QUEENSLAND

It looked like one of the random truck inspection spots that road traffic authorities set up at intervals all over Australia, to check that trucks aren't breaching any of the road rules that apply to them. They operate for a little while, and then close up and move to a new area once the word has spread among the truckies about their presence.

This one, however, had a more specific focus. To the many trucks that sped past it looked as though it was still being set up, but it was in fact ready to go. It was waiting for a signal from an unmarked police car further back up the road that a particular truck was coming, and when that radio call was received the final signs were put in place and an inspection official stood ready to wave the truck in.

The refrigerated truck duly pulled in, the large name of Ioannides Meats visible along both sides. Several inspection officials made the usual checks, of tyres, logbook and so on, and then asked for the back of the truck to be opened. The driver protested that that wasn't normal, but the inspectors insisted.

Inside there were rows and rows of meat carcases, which the inspectors had expected to find. Their interest in them would be the identifying marks to show which properties the carcases had come from. They were recording all the details from each, expecting that a later check at HQ would reveal some of dubious origin. What they hadn't expected to find, however, were two human bodies in one corner of the cargo area.

The truck was immediately impounded and driven away for forensic inspection, and the driver was arrested. The temporary inspection point was then dismantled, and that stretch of highway returned to normal.

And while the truck was in the holding area for further investigation an equally astonishing discovery was made, which resulted in some quick and intensive discussions beyond the confines of the stock squad.

ALAN CAMPBELL

Next morning we were all still of the view that we should call in at Mal Robertson's property. We drove up the same road as yesterday, and on past the entrance to Pascoe Downs. After that the road deteriorated somewhat, though it would still have been passable to smaller trucks coming to collect slaughtered meat.

We found the entrance to Forestview first by the large signs saying "Visitors only by Appointment – No Entry otherwise". It was quite reminiscent of his earlier property that we'd seen, Crystal Park. We figured that Mal's grudging invitation to us when we met him constituted an invitation, so we drove in.

The homestead was simple – another high-blocked Queenslander, but not overdone in any way. We climbed up the stairs and banged on the front door.

It was opened by a male, probably somewhere in his thirties. He looked at us with a bored and slightly hostile expression.

'Yeah?'

No manners at all. However, it didn't take much intuition to work out that his father was almost certainly Mal Robertson

– a physical resemblance as well as the lack of manners.

'Hi, would you be Wayne Robertson by any chance?'

His eyes narrowed further, and he looked quite wary.

'Who's asking?'

'We're from the Department of Primary Industries. We're doing a survey of pest flies of cattle across northern Australia. We met your father at Mount Spec, and he said he'd be happy for us to take samples on any of your family properties.'

'Oh well, I guess that'd be all right then.' He obviously wasn't going to cross his father. 'What do you want to do exactly?'

'Well, if you had at least a rough map of the property, we're particularly keen on any patches of rainforest that might harbour some of the PNG species that are a threat to the north here.' I didn't think I'd add the bit about anywhere that Anna Ioannides might just have been buried. Not that there'd be any sign of that by now, I'm sure.

His eyes had narrowed a bit further at the mention of the forest, but there could have been nothing in that.

'I'll just go and see if I can find a map. Just wait here if you don't mind.'

Something he doesn't want us to see inside? Maybe I'm just getting over-suspicious.

He came back with a sort of map. 'This is a copy I've run off for you – you can take it if you like. There's some forest particularly in this area.'

He pointed to one bit. The map, however, seemed to have several similar patches which he didn't bother about. Don't get over-suspicious, though....

'I should have introduced the rest of the team. This here's Gil Reynolds who's an expert on the breeding stages of the flies, and this here's Nicholas Twistleton who's another expert biologist. Actually, now that I think of it there's one other question that we might ask you. There was a girl who worked in Sydney with Fergus O'Riordan, Nicholas's in-law, for several years – Anna Ioannides. We heard that she'd come up north a little while ago, and we're hoping to catch up with her. You wouldn't have come across her, would you? I don't imagine there's much female company up this way, and I thought you might have met her.'

He was definitely very much on his guard now. He didn't answer straight away, and I reckoned he did know her and he was weighing up whether to make a total denial and risk that we had some other evidence that she'd been here, or make some other evasive answer. It turned out to be the latter.

'I think I remember the name. Was she fairly tall and thin, and had a longish face?'

'That sounds like her.'

'Well she turned up here one day looking for a job. I think she was hitching up the highway, and she must have walked from the main road. I had to say that we didn't have any vacancy for someone like her here. It was a bit late in the day, so we fed her and let her bunk down for the day. Next morning I drove her back to the highway, and she said she'd go on and look somewhere else. Dunno where she went after that.'

It was plausible, but I was sure it was also untrue. However, that was enough for the moment.

'Okay, thank you for your time, and we might go and look at that area of scrub and do a bit of insect-collecting. We might set an insect trap or two and come back and collect the results in a few days' time if that's okay.'

'Sure, you're welcome.'

And with that he turned back and shut the door again.

We looked at each other in silence, then went back to the car. We drove on to the patch of forest, and got out. Gil looked at me.

'Comments?'

'Well, that was about as much bullshit as I'd find anywhere on this property. I don't believe most of what he said, and certainly none of it about Anna Ioannides. Remember that the Mount Carbine caravan park saw him with someone who sounded just like Anna. He also looked nervous when we raised the subject. However, I didn't want to follow up any more at this stage. Let's just have a poke around this forest a bit and Gil can set some traps to give us a reason to come back.'

Nicholas then piped up. He hadn't said much so far on this trip, though I could see him looking keenly at everything around him and listening to what was going on.

'I'm not claiming to be an expert on anything Australian, but I can and do watch people. My university made me a harassment contact officer, and to teach me a few relevant skills they sent me on a course on human awareness or some title like that. They taught us to watch for signs of when people were lying, being unnecessarily nervous, dodging particular topics and so on. I shouldn't be teaching you to do your job, Alan, and you no doubt saw all this too. Wayne Robertson was calm, collected and arrogant until Anna was mentioned. Then he got very twitchy, and he stopped making eye contact with any of us. And all the signs were that he was downright lying when he said he didn't really know her. He was making it up on the go, and not sure what he was really saying.'

'Yeah, thanks Nicholas. I guess I sort of saw that too, but it's good to have your confirmation.'

Gil then said: 'Before we head off, you might like to make a note of that wagon's rego.' He nodded towards a dusty and rather unkempt looking four-wheel drive utility that was standing near the house. 'Just in case you ever need to come back and look for signs that Anna Ioannides was in the vehicle at some stage. Four wheel drive Nissan Navara, rego WR 666, so it obviously belongs to Wayne. Another one of those arseholes who has to show off his initials on his plate.'

We drove off following the map to several patches of jungly forest that Wayne had marked on the map. In doing that we noticed that there were also one or two patches that he hadn't bothered to mark, but we hadn't asked him for every one of them anyway. Finally we selected three areas, and Gil set up and baited traps, skewered them to the ground and left them. Then we returned to the campground at Coen.

Next I thought I should touch base with the colleague that I trusted in Townsville, so I called him on my satellite phone. His news left me stunned, and I turned to the others.

'You won't believe what I've just heard. The stock squad at Rockhampton decided they were going to take a closer look at the meat that Ioannides' Meats are carrying south down the Bruce Highway. They were planning to look at documentation and any visible marks on the meat that might identify its origin, i.e. stolen or legit. They stopped one truck north of Rocky, and in addition to a large number of beef carcases they found two dead humans. This puts a whole new slant on what the hell Ioannides is up to.'

'Bloody hell, what am I getting myself into here?' said Gil. 'This is getting out of my league.'

'This has only recently happened, and at the moment the CIB's trying to find out who the victims were. As soon as they get anywhere on that I'll go down and discuss it all further, but that'll probably be a few days. In the mean time I might go and have a friendly chat with the policeman at Ironbark Creek. See if I can find out more about Wayne Robertson's movements in that area around the time the body was dumped. And if I'm lucky I might find out something about movements of beef carcases in that area as well. I'll just have to keep it low key and make it sound as though he's helping in an official enquiry. I don't want to frighten him off – or alert Wayne Robertson to what we're thinking about.'

GIL REYNOLDS

Over some beers that night in the Coen pub we decided to explore a few more areas of rainforest in this general area, and we agreed that the first should be the Iron Range National Park, which ought to be the most pristine and original area of natural rainforest in the far north.

'I wouldn't be able to set traps there, of course. You've got to get written permission from the National Parks authority, and that can take a while to get. Even with the fuzz breathing down their necks for priority, I shouldn't wonder. However, nobody can stop us just looking around, and if there happened to be a dead animal lying around and my net happened to swish through the air above it and catch a fly or two I don't think there'd be anyone to see. And Alan of course'd be looking at something else at the time and wouldn't notice it.'

'Yeah, I've brought the wrong glasses with me on this trip,' said Alan, with a wink.

We found the main gateway and entered. The park seemed to be a mixture of relatively open savanna and thicker forest.

We found a suitable-looking patch of forest that had a marked walking track going into it, and we parked and walked in.

The forest was quite dark inside, and it took our eyes a moment to adjust. Birds seemed to be calling everywhere, but we couldn't see a single one in the flesh. Likewise there was regular rustling in the vegetation around us. I don't think it was the wind, but we couldn't see what the cause was.

Some way into the forest we had our first stroke of luck. A carcase, and it had a good odour about it. Well, good if you were after maggots in it. The other two guys wrinkled their noses and moved further away. The carcase was a wild pig, and it must have had a fight with another pig and lost. It was badly gashed in several places, and flaps of skin were hanging off it.

I knelt down and began to probe. As I lifted a flap of skin I saw lots of small white bodies wriggling and burrowing further into the flesh to escape the exposure. You beauty! Just what I was after.

Thankfully this morning I'd packed a couple of tubes containing the preservative fluid to pickle the larvae in. I don't always carry that with me unless I'm sure that I'll find larvae, and this was only supposed to be a preliminary look-see today. I got them out of my backpack and settled down with forceps to pull out some larvae. As I was doing that I overheard Alan say to Nicholas: 'I thought policemen had some nasty jobs at times, but this is worse than anything I've ever had to do. All I need to do is call a forensic guy and they do all of that stuff.'

Nicholas said: 'Well, at least the maggots aren't threatening violence of any sort. You must get your share of that at times.'

Alan replied: 'That's true, but we get well trained for that and we're usually wearing protective gear if we expect any trouble.

And I wouldn't say there's no risk to Gil from a stinking carcase like that. God knows what he might catch from it.'

'Don't worry', I called out. 'I'll make sure to share it with you guys if I get it. I'm not selfish.'

I worked over the carcase for about twenty minutes, sampling larvae from as many different parts of the body as I could find them in. Different flies could have laid at different times, or could have preferences for particular body parts or environmental conditions, and I wanted to get the widest range possible.

While I was collecting samples the other two wandered off, but they were back as I finished. Must have been psychic or something.

'Did you find anything else around this area?'

'No corpses or carcases anyway', said Alan. 'It's pretty much the same sort of vegetation all through here.'

'Well, I think we should go back to the campground and I can have a look at what I've managed to collect. I've only got a small hand lens with me, and it's too dark in here to see any detail with that.'

ALAN CAMPBELL

B ack at the campsite Gil started a preliminary examination of his larvae, and I figured it was time for a brew of tea. Nicholas thought the same, so I made it and the two of us sat down. Nicholas hadn't said much so far on the trip, but I knew he'd been keeping his eyes open so I thought I'd find out if he had any useful thoughts.

'So you've been with us for some days now and you haven't been trying yet to teach us to do our jobs better. But have you had any thoughts along those lines?'

He sat for a moment sipping his tea.

'Well, the first answer to that is that I'm certainly not going to try to teach you how to do better. I think you've made good progress already with a pretty tricky crime. But I do have a few overall thoughts which might help a little bit.

'First, I'll tell you where I'm coming from. I do general research, but I'm not a specific crime investigator. However, I did once have exposure to a crime when Marion and I were in South Africa. It was a murder connected with ivory poaching, and the victim was a good friend of ours – a policeman, actually – so we decided to try and help. In the end we found the one bit of evidence that solved the crime, though when I say 'we' I should say Marion alone. I'd managed to get myself expelled from the country just before the breakthrough, by complaining to police when they were beating up black students at a meeting that I was also attending. They didn't take kindly to criticism over there.

'Anyway, back to here. I've been thinking about Gil's initial conclusion that the murder must have happened in Papua New Guinea, and while I can see his reasons for this, after what you've said I think it would have to be plain impossible. I'm not totally familiar with the geography round here, but I know where PNG is in relation to northern Australia, and I just think the logistics of then getting the body back to Australia and out to Ironbark Creek are impossible. For one, the fly larvae in the body would have been further developed by the time the body got here, or they'd have been gone back into the soil to become flies.

'So that didn't happen in my view, but it seemed insoluble until we came up with the thought that the same larvae might be natural in far north Queensland, like here. I thought about that a bit further, and I thought it could definitely fit within the time frame. So I hope Gil comes up with some positives in due course. But with that as a scenario we've also got some other evidence building up.

'I picked up in Townsville that Anna was coming up this way, and that she'd been associating with various males including Wayne Robertson. Several people have also said that Wayne's an unpleasant person in a number of ways. Then when we encountered Wayne he became evasive on the subject of Anna, and told downright lies according to statements made by other people who'd have no reason to lie. So I think there are some big questions to be asked further about Wayne, but what the best way to go about that is, I don't know. You're the expert on that,' he added, grinning at me.

'Thanks, mate, that's a pretty good summary. I wish some of my colleagues could do as well as that. But as far as the third degree on Wayne goes, yes we need to do it but I haven't quite worked out how to handle that one.'

Nicholas obviously had something else to add.

'There are two other things that I don't think we've looked at fully yet. One is the cattle stealing – duffing I think you called it – which seems to be quite widespread and I'd presume is pretty tightly organised. Some people specialise in the thefts and some then do the moving of meat on to meatworks, if it's on the scale that I'm thinking it must be. And is there just a possibility that Ioannides Meats might be involved in the overall coordination of this?'

'That thought had crossed my mind as well.'

'And I'm further guessing that Wayne Robertson might be one of the middlemen, between the stealers and the meatworks?'

'I'm beginning to like the way this is going.'

'And then I'm going to take one more leap, which may well just be fanciful but it's a thought. I think when you first came to Flyblown Downs you said that the local policeman at Ironbark Creek spends most of his time stealing and butchering cattle?'

'I've had that on pretty good authority, but the stock squad's had difficulty pinning him down. He's always got paperwork to show that the meat was legitimately purchased. He's got someone organised to prepare the paperwork, I'm guessing.'

'Well, could Wayne Robertson be a middleman who takes the meat from the policeman and sends it on to a meatworks? And if he is, it means that he probably visits Ironbark Creek relatively often, and if he just happened to have a dead body that he wanted to dispose of away from his family's properties up here, why not take it to Ironbark and bury it there?'

'Hm, you're ahead of me with that one.' I thought for a moment. 'The more I think about that, more I like the idea. Well worth checking out, anyway. I think as soon as we're finished up here we should go back to Flyblown, and I'll drop over and have a chat to the policeman at Ironbark Creek. I can just ask him generally if he knows Wayne – it needn't sound as though I'm suspicious about anything. Just a general enquiry.'

'And very finally there's the matter of the two bodies turning up in Ioannides' truck. I'm afraid I haven't any thoughts on that at all. Did your informant say whether they had wounds or not? Meaning might they have been murder victims?'

'He said that the bodies were unmarked. He couldn't get anything out of the truck driver – he clammed up totally. My guess is that he knew perfectly well that they were there and why, but he's afraid of Ioannides and losing his job or worse if he says anything. But he's probably going to lose his job anyway, if he's prosecuted for illegal carriage of human remains. If not worse if there's violent crime involved.

'Anyway, I want to get away next to speak to the cop at Ironbark Creek, which leaves the question – what are you two guys going to do now?'

Nicholas said: 'Well, if you don't mind I could come back

with you when you go to Ironbark Creek. I'll rejoin Marion at Flyblown Downs. Unless there's anything more that I can do to help you, of course?'

He said that last bit rather sadly. I think he'd been enjoying our investigation from close hand.

'I could certainly drop you back at the camp – no problem. After that I can't really see a role for you at the moment in the investigation. However, you've made some useful and important comments on this trip, and if you don't mind I'd like to be able to consult you any time I think there's something else you might be able to comment on. I can contact you on the satellite phone at Flyblown.'

I hoped that that sounded encouraging enough.

'Fine by me,' said Nicholas.

'And Gil, what are your plans now?'

'Well, first off I'd like to finish looking at the maggots we've collected so far. I can at least give you an answer on those before you go, unless you're off right at this moment. After that I've still got to go round more of the traps that we set and check the maggots out of them. I can phone you with the results of those. And after that, well, there isn't much point in me going back to Flyblown. I'd finished there anyway. I may as well stay up this way and finish the rest of my wider survey.'

'I think we might as well stay here for the rest of the day – we wouldn't get all that far before night comes. If it's okay with you, Nicholas, we can leave early tomorrow morning?'

'Fine by me, certainly.'

'Right, we'll do some packing up while Gil goes where he belongs – among the maggots.'

I didn't think Gil's finger signal was really necessary....

Late that afternoon Gil called us over.

'I've got some news for you. It's a bit qualified at this stage, but I think it's good.'

I rolled my eyes, but I thought I'd better not say anything. I guess he was trying.

'Well, I haven't found the same maggot as those from Anna's body, but I have found what I believe might be the younger stage of that particular maggot, and if that's right it means that that species does occur up here and we can forget PNG.'

'How reliable is that conclusion, Gil?' I was holding my breath.

'Let me just start with a quick further anatomy lesson on maggots. Alan, don't look at me like that. This'll answer your question.

'Almost all flies of the type we're talking about have three stages of development as maggots. The first stage hatches from the egg. It's very tiny, and it has very few characteristics that you can use for identification. The head skeleton's minimal, there are no spiracles at the front end, and those at the back end are very simple – usually two tiny holes with no real features. Sometimes the two are half joined together.

'Then you get the second stage, which starts to have the more detailed characteristics but still not in full. In the case of our maggot, it's the hind spiracles that are the important feature. In the maggots from Anna they had particularly curly slits of a particular pattern, and in that case I would expect the slits of the second stage to be somewhat curly, but not as exaggerated as in the last stage.

'And that's what I've found so far. I've obviously got only half developed maggots because I got them too early, but I can say that their back slits are curlier than any I've ever seen on any other related larvae, where they tend to be quite straight or at most just a little bent. So my fairly strong guess is that they're the same species, and we just need some older larvae to confirm it. And when I go and clear the next lot of traps that's exactly what I should get – they should be just at the right stage of development given the ambient temperature here. So hold your breath a bit longer and I hope and expect to be able to help you.'

'Mate, that's brilliant news. I think that deserves a drink or two. Let's head off to the pub, and the first round's my shout.'

* * *

Early next morning Nicholas and I set off back to Ironbark Creek and Flyblown Downs. I was quite glad of the company – it was a long and rather tedious drive.

We made Atherton on the first day, and stayed in the luxury of a simple but nice motel there. The owner was ethnically Chinese, though he sounded a hundred per cent Aussie. Nicholas asked me about that, and I said the guy would probably have been descended from Chinese miners who'd come to the area a hundred years or more ago. The manager didn't bat an eyelid at our rather ragged appearance, and we managed to spruce ourselves up quite well. The local café in the evening was also a cut up from the tough steaks and chips that we'd been having in the Peninsula pubs.

Next day we headed down to Ravenshoe and turned west

along the Kennedy Highway to Gilbert River, then struck out north-west towards Miranda Downs. We got to Flyblown Downs just after lunchtime, and it almost felt like arriving home. Not that there was any sort of welcome party – they must have all been out in the bush.

I grabbed a snack out of the food that we had with us, and then said to Nicholas: 'I'm going to pop over to Ironbark Creek and have a quiet word with the copper there. I'll just do it by myself – I want to keep it as low key as possible. Just happened to be passing and thought I'd drop in – that sort of thing. Say hi to the others when they get back, and I'll be back before dusk.'

On my way to Ironbark I debated how to handle this one. I didn't want the copper to think I was investigating him – more that I was seeking help from a colleague. And I didn't want him in any way to think I was investigating Wayne Robertson – I'd have to make meat enquiries the focus, and I had an idea of how to go about that.

To my relief he was in when I arrived at the station. There was nobody else in there, and he was sitting at his desk doing some paperwork. Fudging dockets for meat shipments would be my guess.

'G'day, Bill isn't it? I remember you from a course in Brisbane one time. Alan Campbell, if my face doesn't ring a bell.'

'Yeah, I remember you, Alan.'

Not sure whether that was a positive or negative tone of voice. Keep it friendly and neutral.

'So what brings you out to this remote neck of the woods?'

'I've got tied up with some enquiries about meat movements in Queensland. Not cattle duffing – that's the stock squad, of course. This is in confidence, but the stock squad was manning a routine inspection point on the Bruce Highway recently, and one truck they stopped had a whole heap of carcases plus two dead humans. So now the Crime branch has got involved to look into the human carcase side of it. Please don't let that news go outside here, though – it hasn't been released to the press yet.

'Anyway, I was just coming past here after dropping someone off at Miranda Downs, and I remembered you were here now and you'd had some involvement with local movements of meat. I don't know much at all about that sort of thing, and I'd welcome a bit of expert knowledge to explain to me who does what in the trade.'

'Ask away, mate.'

'Okay, how's most of the meat killed and butchered out this way?'

'Depends on how much is being killed at a time. If it's a few beasts the grazier'll do it himself, and most places are set up for at least small-scale butchering. If it's a lot of beasts they'll usually get a contractor in to do it. They've got the necessary equipment, and some of them have small mobile processing plants.'

'Right. Then where would the meat go after that?'

'It usually goes to a wholesaler who'll build up supplies for a bit, then it'll be picked up by a refrigerated semitrailer and taken off to a meat processing works which could be anywhere. Brisbane, Sydney, Melbourne, anywhere. The local wholesaler for this area's at Julia Creek – bit far away, but he's still the closest. There used to be one at Croydon, but it was too isolated and he couldn't keep it operating.'

Now for the bit of strategy. 'Who are the main people in this area who pick up the meat to go to the wholesalers? I wouldn't mind having a chat to one or two of them.'

'Herbie Rudd's one of them, but I know he's in Townsville at the moment. His truck broke down and he's getting it fixed. Klaus Mertens is another – he's based in Croydon, even though the wholesaler there's closed down. They could tell you at the pub there where to find him. Wayne Robertson's another, but he comes from nearer Townsville.'

I let a deliberate gleam of recognition come into my eye. 'He wouldn't be any relation of Mal Robertson, the mayor of Townsville, by any chance would he?'

'Yeah, he's his son.'

'Oh, I met Mal a little while ago when I was helping to organise a quarantine survey of cattle pests up the Peninsula. He's got a number of properties up that way. I think he mentioned that his son does a bit of shifting of meat from his properties.'

'He takes a bit of local stuff from here, as well. I do a bit of spare time butchering myself, when I've got the time, and he takes some of my meat on occasion.'

'Oh, has he been out here recently?'

Please don't let him ask me why I want to know that.

'He was here a coupla months ago, about. I could tell you from the file.'

He dug out a manila folder from one of his drawers.

'I keep a detailed record of all the meat I process and ship, so there's not going to be any fuss about whether there's anything illegal about it all.'

Interesting that he should be quite so specific about that, though knowing the cloud he was under when he was sent up here it didn't totally surprise me. I also know that it would be quite easy to fudge the details – you've just got to have a record that looks convincing.

He dug around in the folder for a moment, and the said: 'Last time he got anything from me was on August the tenth, so about nine weeks ago.'

He indicated the entry in the folder. You beauty! That means we'll have the evidence of his presence here at about the time the body was dumped, if we need it.

'Bugger, I must have only just missed him then. I was up near Miranda Downs again about that time. Anyway, thanks a lot for all that. One last question – would you say that the people who do the small-scale buying and shipping on are an honest lot. Above board?'

Very unlikely, whatever his response, but I was interested to get it.

'Yeah, I'd say they are. I keep an eye on everything like that that goes on around here, and I've never had any trouble or seen anything dodgy.'

No, because you're probably part of it.

'Okay, thanks for that. I'll go and meet with the guy in Croydon if he's there, but it sounds like we should be looking harder at the people at the semitrailer level. That's where the bodies were found, after all. Thanks again, mate – I'll leave you to your paperwork – bane of a copper's life, isn't it? See you.'

'You're right about that. See yah, mate.'

I think I'd pulled that off all right. I'd been watching his face all the while that we were speaking and I didn't see any trace of suspicion about my questions. But you never know with someone with his past – he'd be pretty canny. I'll just have to hope.

I drove back to Flyblown Downs. Everyone was back by then, and I was surprised at the warm welcome they gave me. Unusual when you're police. Nicholas must have told them how well we'd gone up north.

NICHOLAS

I'd enjoyed the trip up north. That was partly seeing the Cape York Peninsula and a bit of its flora and fauna, although I didn't get to see a tree kangaroo or a bird of paradise. It was partly also the chance to see a little bit of a criminal investigation. When Marion and I had had our involvement with poaching in Africa, our involvement was more like a research project than crime-busting.

Marion seemed pleased to have me back, and I'd certainly missed her company. She might be feisty at times, but she's always good value. She was in a good mood anyway because her research was showing some quite interesting results. It looks as though the grant sponsors might be quite pleased with her outcome. At least one of us might score in that regard, anyway.

Alan Campbell arrived back and gave us a brief report on his chat with the policeman at Ironbark Creek. I sensed that he felt he owed us something, but he didn't want to reveal too much at this stage. I guess we'll hear more in due course.

ALAN CAMPBELL

I drove back to Brisbane the quickest way – not that it was quick by anyone's standard. South to Cloncurry, down the Landsborough Highway to Charleville and the due east to Brisbane. It was a tedious drive solo, but I was thinking all the way of how best to progress this investigation.

Back in Brisbane I thought I'd better find out what had been happening since I'd been away. I called a mate who'd been in the police force longer than I had, and we agreed to meet for a beer in a pub not usually frequented by cops.

'G'day, Lenny. How's tricks?'

'Much the same as usual, mate. Nothing happens when you're not here. No connection, of course.'

'Well, I do try to oblige. I'll see what I can do now that I'm here. You heard anything on the grapevine about the two bodies that were found in the meat semi coming south?'

'Ah, well, maybe there has been something happening after all. Yeah, that caused a bit of a stir for sure. But it looks like it's not as sensational as we all first thought. The bodies came from a funeral home in the north and were being sent back to Melbourne. They died of natural causes, and the funeral director was getting them down there on the cheap. Having charged his full fee for transporting them, of course.

'And the freight company's going to cop it too. It's of course totally illegal to carry human corpses in shipments of meat. The driver's maintaining he didn't know the bodies were in there, but I don't think anybody believes that. The foreman at the depot that shipped it's been questioned pretty hard, but nobody's quite worked out yet whether he was the sole instigator, paid by the funeral home, or whether this came from a higher source in the company. Also whether or not such things have happened before.

'The truck belongs to Ioannides Meats and I think they're going to get the Vics to interview old man Ioannides himself, though I can tell you now what he's going to say and it's probably going to be hard to pin anything directly on to him.'

'So the other aspect of interest's what marks there were on the meat in the shipment in that truck?'

'Yeah, but I haven't heard anything about that. Your best bet's to chat to David Schiller in the Stock Squad. He's a mate of mine. I'll call him and tell him you're a bastard but not a bad sort of a bastard.'

'Thanks, mate – I'll owe you for this one. Another beer?'

'Thought you'd never ask....'

* * *

David Schiller suggested that we meet in the station – he can't have thought there'd be any problem with us getting together. When I met him I wondered whether he would ever have a problem with anyone – he was built like Charles Atlas, and looked and moved super-fit. I certainly wouldn't be taking him on physically.

'G'day, Alan – I've heard about you apart from what Lenny told me – pleasure to meet you at last.'

His voice was surprisingly mild – I'd expected a deep boom.

'Lenny probably told you what I'm interested in, but he wouldn't have known why. And I'd like to say at the outset that I'm not trying to muscle in on the Stock Squad's cases. It's just that my current one overlaps with yours and I reckon we might both benefit from sharing info.'

'Fine by me. Fire away.'

'Okay, my case relates to a body dug up at Coolabah Creek in the Gulf Country. The body was Anna Ioannides, one of the daughters of Nicos Ioannides of the Melbourne meat empire, and she'd been strangled. However, the forensic evidence suggests that she was murdered farther north, probably up the Cape York Peninsula, and her body was taken several days later to Coolabah Creek.

'Anna was a feisty girl. She hated her father's guts, and he wasn't all that impressed with her. She regularly had relationships with men, and equally regularly dumped them after a while, not always very politely. I guess that any of them could have lost it and killed her, but there's very little direct evidence pointing at anyone. However, there is one person who had a recent and particular association with her – Wayne Robertson, the son of the mayor of Townsville.

'This is where it could get interesting in relation to livestock. The Robertsons have a number of cattle stations in the north, and there's anecdotal evidence that they're also involved in cattle duffing in the same area and that some of the dodgy meat goes to Ioannides. Anna could have offended Wayne by dumping him, but it's also conceivable that she could have found out about the duffing and threatened to expose the whole thing. As I said, she was at daggers drawn with her father.

'We also have some evidence indicating that Wayne Robertson went to Ironbark Creek, which is near Coolabah Creek, at about the time when Anna's body was dumped there. Before that he was also up the Peninsula, with Anna, and he lied to us about his involvement with her up there. One other player, who's probably also involved in the meat side but not I would think with the murder, is Bill McIntyre, the copper at Ironbark Creek. You'd probably know about his reputation. Wayne regularly collects meat from him, and I'd be very surprised if the meat isn't stolen.

'So this is where you come in, because I imagine you know a hell of a lot more than I do about the dodgy meat operations. I'm not looking to sort your cases out, though if I find anything useful I'll pass it on to you, but I'd welcome any help with our case because I'm buggered if I can get much hard evidence.'

'Well, you've certainly got a nice can of worms there. And so have we, with the duffing and the movement of dodgy meat around the state and wider. The evidence indicates that it's much more widespread than we'd previously realised, and it involves significant quantities of meat. Nicos Ioannides is almost certainly the biggest receiver of the stolen meat, but he's very smart and keeps himself and the company well covered. Did you, by the way, hear of the recent Ioannides truck that was intercepted on the Bruce Highway and was found to be carrying two human bodies as well as a load of beef?'

'Yeah, even up north I heard about that. But I gather the bodies were being shifted on behalf of a funeral director, to save him money?'

'That's right. It was pure chance that we found them. We organised the stopping of the truck because we wanted to check the markings on the meat they were carrying – the stiffs were an unexpected bonus. Ioannides denies any involvement with or knowledge of the bodies. He says it's just a rogue driver making some extra cash for himself. Hard to prove anything else. Personally I suspect that Ioannides was fully aware and was taking the profit, but it was careless of the operators to do it because it means we're now much more focused on what they're doing.

'Our main interest has been in markings on the shipped meats, because we've had increasing evidence that there's quite a few fake ones around. They look like normal meat IDs, but there's no property or abattoir that relates to them. Nobody would pick them up from a casual glance, though a wholesaler or meatworks would look more carefully and spot the problem. Unless they were crooked operators, of course. Can't think of who I might be implying there, of course.

'The other problem we're beginning to get a handle on is genuine ID marks but some of them have been applied to meat that must have come from other sources, e.g. cattle duffing. That's where we particularly have Mal Robertson in our sights. We've done some tallies and found that his properties could only have turned off about a third of the amount of meat that's labelled with his mark – the rest has come from somewhere else. So we certainly have a common interest in that area.

'We have knowledge that Wayne Robertson's a principal

buyer of meat from a lot of places around the Gulf, including from Bill McIntyre who runs a sideline in meat butchering and trading. All totally above board of course, and he's very careful to have paperwork to cover everything that he does. Half of that's fake too, I'm sure, but we haven't caught him out yet. You'd know his reputation in the force when he got shunted off to Ironbark Creek, of course?'

'Yeah, pretty well, actually.'

'So what we wouldn't mind doing when we've got a bit more evidence of who's doing what on a significant scale is do some targeted snap raids to try to pick up unmarked meat and things like that. But there's one complicating factor. Are you aware of a dimension of drug smuggling also involved?'

'I've picked up some preliminary comments. I've been warned not to go in heavy myself, but to consult with the Feds who're taking the running on that. I've been given the name of a key contact, but I haven't had time to touch base with him yet. I haven't seen any evidence of drugs being involved during our investigations, but I probably wouldn't anyway.'

'Well, what I'm about to tell you now is in absolute confidence. When the truck was in the police garage for its further inspection of the contents, by pure chance a drug sniffer dog happened to go past on its way to sniff another vehicle. However, as it went past the meat truck it went ballistic, and it was showing enormous interest in what appeared to be one of the fuel tanks along the side of the truck. You know how some of the big rigs have large rectangular fuel tanks along the sides. Anyway, on further inspection they found that it wasn't a fuel tank at all. It was a dummy stuffed full of drugs, and it was a pretty large amount. The stock squad immediately contacted the Feds, who are full on with that side of the investigation. It's heavily under wraps at the moment. They haven't told Ioannides about that discovery, and the driver doesn't know either. He's still being held on the charge of transporting human bodies illegally, but he thinks that's all at the moment. The Feds are currently working out how they can capitalise on this discovery, and they're keeping everyone else ignorant of the fact that they know about the drugs.

'So we should sit down and start some planning to see how our two investigations could work together, but we'll definitely have to get the Feds in on any meetings now. Otherwise we risk planning something that would then cause problems when we went ahead. I'll give my contact a call now.'

'All makes sense to me, mate – let's go for it.'

GIL REYNOLDS

Peace descended as Alan and Nicholas left, though after a while it was actually too quiet. Alan could be a bit full on, but I'd enjoyed watching him work. Especially how he interacted with people to achieve what he wanted. Nicholas was also good company – quieter, but he had a nice wry sense of humour.

However, they were all relying on me to come up with the definitive answer on the maggots with the curly spiracles, and I guess Anna was too if she was going to have any chance of justice.

I still had various traps set in several bits of forest, but my first task was to set up rudimentary facilities for processing the material that I'd be collecting. I needed a small bench somewhere where I could set up some small cages for breeding flies out of baits, and another where I could set up a microscope for preparing and dissecting maggots and a tray on which to lay out microscope slides as I prepared them and dried them. The first one could be anywhere, but the second needed a power source for the light on the microscope.

I thought of Ray Smith at Pascoe Downs. He seemed interested in our investigation, and if I ask him not to talk too much about it I'm sure that wouldn't worry him. Then maybe I could get a room in the Coen pub that his brother runs, and that should be okay for setting up a microscope.

I drove over to Pascoe and found Ray about to drive down to the paddocks. I asked him if he might have a shed or something where there was a flat surface on which I could set up cages for rearing flies.

'No problem at all, mate. I've got a couple of sheds that aren't getting much use at the moment.'

'There'd be a bit of smell, I'm afraid. The meat for rearing the flies would be somewhat off. None of the flies would get out – they're all inside sealed cages, but there would be some stink.'

'Mate, there's plenty around a cattle property that stinks, too. The sheds are well away from the house, anyway, so the missus won't be complaining.'

He took me over and showed me both. Either would have done, so I picked the one with the most bench space. The door had a padlock, and he handed me the key.

'Come and go any time you like. You won't be bothering us. Come over and meet me dogs, and then they won't bother you either when they see you here.'

We went over to his ute, which had two dogs in the back. The dogs leapt around with excitement.

'Hey, steady, boys. This one here's Rough, from the noise he makes too much of the time, and the brindle one's Tarzan. That came from when he was a pup, and he picked up this giant bone and made off with it. Okay, boys, say hello to Gil. He's a friend, orright?'

The two dogs jostled with each other to see which of them could lick my hand the hardest, but they seemed happy enough.

'Right, mate, I'll leave you to it. I'm happy to be able to do something to help with all this. It's a bad business.'

I thought I'd go first and see if there was a room in the Coen pub that would be okay for setting up a microscope, and come back here later to get some cages ready. When I got to the pub it had finished its dinner rush, if there had been one, and the publican was cleaning up the bar.

'G'day, Stu. We met the other day when I was through with a couple of others. You'll probably remember we were asking about a young lass who had come up this way. And if you've been talking to your brother Ray you'll probably have heard that one of my mates was a cop and is investigating the murder of the girl.'

'Yair, he did say something about it.'

I knew he would have. The outback may be relatively empty, but word still travels around fast.

'I'm doing one part of the investigation which involves looking at insects picked up from the study. Ray's lent me one of his sheds to process the smellier part of the operation, but I need to have somewhere to set up a microscope to look at what we've managed to collect. I wondered whether you'd have a room that I could use? No smell, no mess – just a flat surface to set the instrument up on, with a power point accessible because the scope's got a light on it.'

'No problem at the moment – we're out of the busy season. You'd want a single room not a shared one, obviously. None of them have got their own bathroom up this way, but the main bathroom wouldn't be far from any of them.'

'That sounds good. I'd like to keep what I'm doing fairly quiet – I wouldn't want to have anything that'd cause a problem if I had to give evidence about it in a court. Would the room cleaner be okay with that?'

'Mate, you'll get Elsie. She's been cleaning here for the last fifteen years or so, and she's as good as any you'd ever get. Better than half the flighty ones in the big cities, too. I'll show you what'd probably be the best room for what you want, and if it's okay you can sign the register and I'll give you the key.'

The room turned out to be fine, so I brought my gear up and set the microscope up. Then some trays on which to put newly-prepared microscope slides while they dried. I left the components for my cages in the car – it would be easier to assemble them in Ray's shed than to put them together here and have to carry them made up.

There wasn't much left of the day, so I wandered down to the bar, sat in a corner and started to watch the outback world go by.

I was on my second beer when there was an interesting arrival at the bar. It was unmistakably Wayne Robertson, with a young girl in tow. He was too busy trying to impress her to look around the rest of the bar, but I doubted that he'd have recognised me even if he had. He'd focused mainly on Alan when we met him.

His interactions with the female confirmed my impression of him as a prize sleaze. If I'd been her I'd have given him a good slap across the face several times, but she seemed happy enough with him. I hoped that this encounter didn't turn out to be like Anna's, if we were right about our suspicions.

After a while – and a number of drinks – Wayne and

companion went off again, and I went into the dining room for a meal. Steak was the only item on the menu tonight, but it wasn't as tough as some that we'd had up this way, and the chips were nicely fresh and light.

* * *

Next morning after an early breakfast I was off to Ray's shed to make up my cages. My lab had made up some neat kits that were light and easily portable. There were twelve lengths of thin metal rod and eight corner pieces that the rods slotted into. The whole made up a cube shape, and there was a sleeve of insect netting that fitted over the whole. The sleeve had one hole for access, which got tied up while there were flies in it. I didn't know how many I'd need so I made up all twelve that I'd brought.

Then it was off to inspect the various traps and bait animals that I'd left out before. That took the rest of the day because I had to travel between the several sites, but a cursory glance at what I was picking up looked quite encouraging. I got them back to Pascoe Downs and set everything up in the cages and on the benches, and then went back to the pub.

No sign of Wayne Robertson that evening – no sign of people much at all. No wonder Stu had said it wasn't the high season. I went into the dining room for the evening meal, which was – you guessed it – steak and chips. The chips were as good as ever, but the steak was a bit tougher than the last one.

Well, you can't win 'em all….

ALAN CAMPBELL

David Schiller had managed to get hold of his Federal Police contact quickly, and the contact seemed pretty keen to meet with us as soon as possible. Maybe an indication of how important their investigation was to them.

The three of us met next morning in a small back office in the Police headquarters in Brisbane.

'Alan, this is Merv Tansley of the Australian Federal Police. Merv, Alan Campbell of the Queensland Police. Murder and Serious Crimes, and as I told you he's investigating the murder of a young girl in north Queensland. A Person of Interest in his case is Wayne Robertson, at which point I think I can pass over to you to put your angle on Wayne. And I should let you know that I've told Alan in confidence about your extra discovery in the meat truck. I can vouch a hundred percent for his security on this.'

'G'day, Alan, pleased to meet you. Yeah, I've got a major interest in north Queensland at the moment, from the point of view of illegal drugs entering Australia. We've picked up quite a lot of indirect evidence that drugs are coming in regularly at some point in the north, possibly the very far north, but so far we haven't got any hard evidence of who, how and where. Until very recently we hadn't made any interceptions, either. Not for want of trying, I can tell you, but whoever's doing it is professional and careful.

'We've been trying to pinpoint possible points of entry, such as safe marine landing areas and places where a plane might be able to touch down. There aren't too many of the latter. There's an old wartime landing strip up at Iron Range, but it's pretty overgrown. We've installed a surveillance camera there but it hasn't picked anything up yet. There are commercial airports at Weipa and Thursday Island, but it'd be relatively hard to get anything through there without being detected sooner or later. Several cattle stations also have their own landing strips, and they'd be the easiest to use. They're relatively well maintained, and flights in and out wouldn't be noticed by many people. The graziers themselves fly in quite often – people would just assume it's them.

'So we've been trying to watch people who regularly go between cattle stations and places further south, who could be carrying drugs. A couple of people are on our radar, and one of them's Wayne Robertson. His family has several properties that are in the right area – the only problem is that none of them have airstrips. He could be picking up shipments from neighbours or from landing points, of course, but we haven't got any evidence of that so far. However, one of their properties at Iron Range is relatively near the Portland Roads jetty. We've also got covert surveillance there now, but so far nothing.

'The other reason that Wayne's of interest is that he's a regular at night clubs and discos in Townsville, especially one called Screwball which covert surveillance has indicated is a major place for drugs changing hands.

'We still don't know the points of entry, but we've now picked up this one large shipment going south. I can tell you also that it was a very professional operation. The drug container looked exactly like a vehicle fuel tank, and it was only the sheer luck that the drug dog went past at the right moment and detected it. I'm hoping that we might now get closer to hard results, but nobody's saying anything at this stage.

'We decided that if we didn't let on to anyone that we'd made this discovery they might simply continue doing the runs but we'd now be watching for what happens. We had to get pretty high authority to allow such an amount of drugs to go without interception, but they could see the logic so we got it. You can see now why we wouldn't want you to do anything in your investigation that might alert people too much and prejudice ours.'

Put your clod-hopping boots into the mix was what he meant, but he was tactful enough not to say it.

'Our thought at this stage is that we might install trackers on at least some of Ioannides' trucks that do the regular run to north Queensland. We'll pick up where they collect their meat cargo from, but a tracker would tell us if they go to any other places to pick up a drug container before they come south again. That's why we haven't told either Ioannides or the driver that we know about the drugs, in the hope that that side of their operation will continue.

'The other thing we're planning to do is put full time surveillance on Wayne Robertson from now on, to see if we can find out more about what's coming in where. We can't guarantee that he's involved, but I'd put good money on it. We're also going to keep a bit of an eye on his father, Mal Robertson. He may or may not know what his son's doing, but I'd be surprised if he's totally ignorant. He's known in the north as a wheeler dealer. So both of those surveillances might also yield some information on the meat trading for you guys. That's not our primary aim, of course, but we'll be keeping full notes of absolutely everything that Wayne does, and to a lesser extent Mal, and of course we'll pass anything relevant on to you.

'Now, what do you guys plan on doing on your side?'

Dave Schiller spoke. 'I think in the light of what you've just told us we'll have to go away and have a further discussion on our own angles. I'm of course interested in any of the meat trading side, but remember that Alan's got a murder enquiry under way, and Wayne Robertson's a prime suspect in that. But as soon as we've worked something out we'll let you know. Before we take any action' he added with a grin.

'No problems, mate. We'll look forward to hearing from you. Cheers, David, cheers Alan. Good luck.'

I wasn't sure how much was left unsaid in all of that, but Dave and I could sort it all out over a beer or two.

GIL REYNOLDS

I was sitting in my hotel room when a knock came at the door.
I called out to come in, and the door opened to reveal a middle-aged aboriginal woman.

'Hi, you must be Elsie?'

'That's my whitefeller name, yeh. Anyway, welcome to Kaantju country.'

'Thank you. I pay my respects to your ancestors, and I acknowledge your ownership of this country.'

'Well, well. We don't get too many people up this way who know the traditional greeting. You've worked with aboriginal people before, mate?'

'Not me so much, but my father did a lot in Brisbane, and he trained me.'

'Well, he done okay then. Stuey said you was all right. Anyway, okay if I clean your room now, or would you like me to come back?'

'Now'd be fine. Come in.'

She entered wheeling her cleaning trolley in front of her.

'Stuey said I had to be careful of your things in here.'

'It's just these bits here,' I said, pointing at the microscope and the slides that I'd just begun to lay out.

'Oh, you must be one of them insect fellers, with that microscope and the glass slides.'

'Gee, you're on the ball with that. How do you know about all this?'

'Well, a coupla years back we had two fellers staying here who were doing the same. They was looking for fruit flies – nasty ones that might have come in from PNG. My cousins helped 'em a bit. Them fellers was collecting different fruits to see what flies were in 'em. They knew how to find mangoes and bananas and fruits like that, but they didn't know nothin' 'bout most of the native fruits. Blackfellers know all about them. We've been collectin' 'em and eatin' 'em since forever. My cousins went out into the forest and gathered all sorts of wild fruits. The fellers was very grateful.'

'Okay, you're right that I'm up here collecting insects, but mine are ones that attack cattle. I'm especially watching out for a thing called screwworm. It's not here but it's in PNG, and if it gets in here it'll do a lot of damage to all our cattle.'

'Yeah, my cousin Chaz at Pascoe Downs told me 'bout that one. He's a stockman there, and his boss Ray told him to watch out for 'em. They eat holes in the sides of the cattle, he said.'

'That's right. I've seen them in PNG and they're very nasty.' I paused. 'You sound like you'd have made a good insect person yourself.'

'I wouldn't have minded, but there aren't too many chances for blackfellers from up here to go to university. Anyway, I'm a bit old now.'

'Yeah, I can understand the problem but it's very sad. If

you'd like to clean in here now that's fine by me. Just miss this bit, and I'll do it myself if I make any mess.'

Elsie started cleaning and I went back to labelling slides. Then a thought suddenly crossed my mind from something she'd said.

'You said your cousin's a stockman at Pascoe Downs. He'd probably know the folks at the next-door property, Forestview, would he?'

Her face screwed up. 'Huh, them fellers. Yeah, we all know 'em around here and we wish we didn't. Thieving bastards. My cousin's seen 'em a few times pulling down fences to let Ray's animals through on to their property. When he's said that, they say he's wrong, he's only a blackfeller – the fence was down anyway and they was trying to fix it but the stock got through. They didn't know he actually saw them. Whitefellers of that sort don't notice blackfellers.'

'Would you know one of them called Wayne Robertson?'

'We all know him round here, and he's the worst of the lot. He thinks he's God, and he doesn't like blackfellers. Abos and boongs, he calls us. He's in the bar here quite a lot, and it usually means trouble. He's often got some young sheila with him, and I don't think they know what they're in for. He had one here a coupla months back. She was a feisty one and she was giving him plenty of backchat. I could see he didn't like that. I help in the bar quite often – that's when I saw them.'

'That sounds like the lass who got herself killed not long after.'

'Jeez, that's bad. I didn't hear about that.'

'Look, I'd better not hold you up too much or you'll be in trouble.'

'No worries, Stuey won't mind. As long as I gets me work done he doesn't mind when, and there's not too many in the pub at the moment. I've just got to get to the kitchen before lunchtime. I help the cook a bit with things.'

She cleaned around the room quickly and efficiently. Then as she was about to leave she said:

'Look, mate, can I give you one bit of advice? You've got them insects stuck on pins there. The other blokes I was telling you about did that, and they left 'em on the bench like you've done and they went out for a while. When they came back there was hardly an insect left on the pins. The bloody little ants had got in and eaten 'em all. They had to go out and collect a whole lot more, and the next time they stood the tray of insects inside another tray with water in it. The ants can't get across the water. I reckon you should do the same.'

'Jeez, Elsie, thanks for that tip. I'll have to get hold of a water tray somewhere. Maybe the shop up the road'll have something.'

'I can probably find you something in the kitchen if you like. They won't mind. Just wait here a minute.'

She went off and returned in a few minutes with two enamel trays that were the right size for one to fit inside the other. She put them on the bench, then went off wheeling her trolley along the corridor.

I was beginning to like Elsie.

* * *

In the afternoon I went back to Pascoe Downs to check what had emerged from my baits in the cages I'd set up there. There were some quite interesting looking flies – a greater diversity than I'd expected. I put sugar, water and a bit of stock for protein in the cages so the flies would feed and harden off their body skeletons. If you pin flies while they're soft, all you finish up with is a shrivelled mess which you can't identify. A few days of feeding them up and I should be able to process them all.

I was still thinking of Elsie, who wasn't at all what I'd been expecting for a room maid, when a further thought crossed my mind. She'd mentioned that her cousin at Pascoe Downs used to see what went on with their Robertson neighbours because the white guys didn't take much notice of blackfellers around, presumably because they didn't regard them as important so they ignored them. However, I knew that aboriginals were extremely good observers themselves – that was how they'd survived and hunted for thousands of years – and I wondered whether we could use these skills to follow up the other line of the police enquiry, namely the drug importations. Should I raise it first with Alan, or should I sound Elsie out myself? I couldn't decide.

I lay in bed that night pondering it further, and decided that I'd make a tentative approach to Elsie when she came in that morning, and see what sort of reception it got.

* * *

By the next morning I'd worked out how I was going to approach Elsie. I went down for breakfast, and who should be serving there but Elsie. I should have guessed.

'Morning, Elsie – how are you?'

'I'm good, thanks for asking. And yerself?'

'I'm good too, thanks to you looking after me.' I said it with a grin, and got a faint one back. 'Will you be doing my room again today?'

'Yeah, I do 'em every day.'

'I've got something I'd like to ask you. What time do you think you might be in?'

'I could do you first if you like. 'Bout half past nine – I've got to do the washing up from here first.'

'Great – see you then.'

When Elsie arrived and brought her cleaning gear in I said: 'You know I said yesterday that I was interested in things being brought in from overseas that could be dangerous to health here. Like food with diseases in it, or fruits with fruit flies – things like that. Government people like me don't know the area all that well, and we aren't here all the time, so all sorts of things could be going on that we never find out about. But your people are the experts on everywhere and everything around here, and you'd see things that a whitefeller wouldn't ever see. Would you be able to ask your people if they do ever notice anything like that that seems odd?'

'Yeah, I could ask the aunties. There's a few of them around the place. Dunno that they'd have seen food and fruit and stuff like that, though. Main thing I've heard 'em talk about is drugs that get brought in. They don't like that because the people who bring 'em in sell 'em to our young people. Causes all sorts of problems, that does.'

I tried to suppress any look of amazement on my face. The very thing I wanted to find out, and it was offered to me, just like that.

'Yeah, I can see why they'd be worried about that. I hate

drugs too – I've seen what they can do to people, and not just the folks who take them. The people who bring them in could be bringing all sorts of stuff in, and I'd be very interested if your aunties could give me any more information about what's actually happening.'

'No problem, I can ask them. Might take me a few days, but.'

'That's all right. I'll be here for some days yet, and I can always come back if you don't have anything before I go.'

* * *

That evening a quick phone call (not overheard by anyone else) brought Alan up to speed with Elsie's dramatic announcement.

Alan did some quick thinking, and then said: 'We'd better stick to your schedule. I wouldn't want to try to rush Elsie in any way or we might blow the whole thing. Stay up there as long as you need. If your budget won't cover the hotel cost we can help you out.'

'That's unusually generous of the Queensland Police.'

'Who said anything about Queensland Police? We'll charge it to the Feds – they've got more money than we have. Anyway, if you do have to leave make sure that you do get back up to Elsie, and keep me posted as things develop.'

He paused, then said: 'You're almost justifying your involvement in all this, you know. I might even buy you a beer next time I see you.'

'Stuff that, mate! No beer this time. I reckon if we can crack this, it'll be at least a bottle of champagne…'

ALAN CAMPBELL

In the light of what Gil Reynolds had reported from Coen, Merv Tansley of the Feds was very keen to meet again with me and Dave Schiller. He opened the batting.

'That was great news that your mate up north told you. It's likely confirmation that drugs are coming in up there, and also that Wayne Robertson is very likely to be involved. I mentioned last time we met that we were starting surveillance on Wayne, but we're upping that now. We'll be putting a tracker on his vehicle, which you'd identified for us. There may be the odd moment when there's no satellite up that way to pick up the signals, but the coverage even up there's pretty good these days and we should get a reasonably clear picture of his movements and in particular where he stops for a significant period of time.

'We've also decided to put a similar tracker on any vehicles owned by Wayne's father, Mal. I'd have trouble believing that Wayne's doing everything by himself – it's all too organised. I reckon Mal would at the very least know about it, and he may have more or less of a role in it.

'And as I told you earlier, we've decided to put trackers on at least some of Ioannides' meat trucks that do the northern run. Our best estimate from logs kept by the Department of Main Roads at their routine highway checks is that he has eight large trucks that service the north regularly. They have to stop at the check points when they pass them. They won't be suspicious, and while the main check's being done one of our guys can fasten a tracker on where it won't be found. We won't do all the trucks – maybe three, maybe four.

'We'll see them stop at the meat processing place to load the main cargo, but hopefully at least some of them will go regularly to another place as well. We could then put some other form of surveillance on that place too.

'And, needless to say I'm busting a gut to know if that Elsie comes back to Gil Reynolds with anything more.'

GIL REYNOLDS

I spent the next ten days systematically clearing traps, collecting maggots, rearing out adult flies, pinning them and trying to identify the species. By the end of the time I had a number of different fly species, but none of them looked as closely like *Calliphora aiyurensis* as I'd hoped. However, I was only going on written descriptions of *aiyurensis*, and that was never easy. There was only one thing for it – to look at some actual specimens of *aiyurensis* for comparison with what I'd got. I'd also take down the maggots that had come from Anna Ioannides' body.

I called the National Museum of Victoria, and this time thank God the fly expert was there. He checked his collection of PNG material and called me back to say that he had some excellent specimens of *aiyurensis*, so I told him to hang on to them at all costs and I'd be down as soon as I could to see them.

Then I called Alan Campbell and explained the situation. He responded as I'd expected.

'This is going to cost us money, right?'

'You want conclusive evidence for your murder enquiry, too right. Cheap at the price, I'd have thought.'

'So what will we be up for?'

'Well, I could drive from Coen to Melbourne if you can wait for a week or so, and then another week to get back. Or I could drive from Coen to Cairns and get a plane from there to Melbourne, or I could get a Bush Pilots plane from Coen to Cairns and then fly on from there. Bush Pilots are leaving from here at six tomorrow morning. Would you have time to authorise both flights before then?'

'Outside my financial delegation, mate – I'll have to check and call you back.'

He rang back about half an hour later. His department must have been taking this seriously because he said: 'All done, from Coen to Melbourne. They'll probably cut my salary to pay for it, but at least I can think of you getting up at sparrow fart tomorrow morning to catch the plane. I happen to know the airport's about 20 k's north of Coen, along a slow road.'

Next I went to look for Elsie, who was doing some cleaning up in the kitchen. Luckily nobody else was around at the time.

'Hi Elsie. You know that matter I was talking to you about earlier. I've got to go south to check some fly specimens in somebody else's collection, but I'll be back in four or five days. I'll ask Stuey to keep my room for me, and I'll be just as keen to know anything you've found out when I get back.'

'No worries, mate. I'll still be here. I've got a few enquiries out, but I haven't heard nothin' back yet. I haven't forgotten.'

Then I went and organised with Stuey for me to hang on to the room with my gear in it. Then I went to pack some things for a quick trip to Melbourne. The most important was to take as many pinned flies and larvae as I could carry with me, so that I'd get the best comparison that I could. I could feel a tingle of excitement coming on.

* * *

One of the good things about Bush Pilots is that they don't hang about. They load the bags as people arrive at the small airport, and it doesn't take long to get the passengers on board either. We were off on the dot of six, landed once at Musgrave Station, and then we were in Cairns. Plenty of time for my onward trip to Melbourne, via Brisbane.

Next morning I was at the National Museum of Victoria right on opening time. I'd met my contact there, Giles Roback, at a conference only a few months earlier, so we could get straight down to business. He sat me down at a long bench and brought out all the material of blowflies that they'd got from Papua New Guinea. I immersed myself in it all – bliss.

By morning teatime I was sure that none of the specimens that I'd so far got from the Iron Range area were *Calliphora aiyurensis*. The most reliable features for distinguishing flies are the number and layout of bristles on the top of the fly's thorax, the layout of spines on the legs, and the surface patterning – the patterns of stripes on the thorax, and the layouts of dark spots on the abdomen. The ones I'd got so far had no variation between any of these characters across all the specimens, and neither did the *aiyurensis* ones, but there were significant differences between mine and *aiyurensis*. However, I hadn't yet got the full range of adults, so I contented myself with making detailed notes of *aiyurensis* and photographing the Victorian specimens as well as I could.

I had a quick morning coffee with Giles, and then got him to search his collection of maggots for the *aiyurensis* from PNG that I knew he had. And when I compared my maggots that had come from Anna Ioannides' body with his *aiyurensis*, it was quite clear that I had something fairly like *aiyurensis* but definitely not exactly the same. There were two good sets from PNG to compare against Anna's. On the hind spiracles Anna's had distinctly more wiggles on each respiratory slit than the PNG ones, the small holes called buttons were in slightly but consistently different positions, and the overall shape of the plate on Anna's was more elongate than the PNG ones. I would have no doubt at all in testifying in a court that the maggots from Anna Ioannides were not *Calliphora aiyurensis* from Papua New Guinea. But what I still needed was to find Anna's one in far North Queensland. Yet more collecting and sampling....

Anna's maggots must be a new and undescribed species, since there are no records of anything like it in the literature, nor in any of the insect collections that I'd studied, which covered most of them around Australia. It's not unusual to find new species in remote areas, however – many areas haven't been all that well surveyed unless a particular expert happened to collect in the location.

I immediately rang Alan Campbell.

'Hi Alan. I'm currently in Victoria at the National Museum, and I can confirm to you beyond any doubt that the maggots from Anna Ioannides weren't the species from Papua New Guinea. They're a closely related but distinct species that's probably indigenous to far north Queensland, and I'd testify to that in court. Worth the cost of my trip down here?'

'Thanks, mate. That's one step forward, certainly. God knows how anyone could have come up with such a hare-brained notion that she was killed in PNG, of course, but these things happen when you're dealing with scientists. But we've still got one problem. We've got a reasonably likely suspect in Wayne Robertson, but absolutely no evidence on which to charge him. So in the present run of things you won't be having to testify in court anyway.'

'Yeah, I do realise that, but I'm hoping that now that investigations have intensified something might turn up.'

'Well, we might be able to get him for dodgy dealings to do with meat, or even possibly for involvement with drugs, but we'll be mighty lucky to get anything on the murder.'

I said: 'There was one thought that crossed my mind, though. I think the pathology report said that Anna's body must have been moved from its initial resting place at least three days and probably four after her death. She would already have had some rot set in, and the body was also significantly gouged by something or someone – probably wild pigs. My guess is that if it was Wayne he simply loaded her into the back of his ute and threw some tarps over her. Where he was travelling there'd have been very little chance of anyone seeing anything. It's possible then that the damaged body shed a bit of tissue on to the ridges in the ute's tray, or on to the tarp itself, and it's just possible that some might be left there. My memory of Wayne's ute is that it's pretty messy, so one could always hope. What the chances would then be of getting DNA off them I don't know, but experts can do magic things.'

'Okay, I can see where you're coming from. I'll have to discuss this with the others, though. We're trying to avoid any obvious signs of our investigations at the moment, because if we wade in on one front, like the murder, it may prejudice the investigations of the meat and/or the drugs. The Feds'll kill me if I stuff up the drug one. I don't know how long DNA lasts, and Wayne might suddenly decide to give his ute a thorough clean, but I think we'll just have to take that risk. There mightn't be any there anyway.'

'Well, I think I'll get back to the north now. I've done all I can on the Anna maggot angle. I may as well now finish my survey of all the blowflies up in that area, which is what I'm employed to do, and I still need to find the actual fly that produces Anna's maggots. Also I'd like to be around if Elsie comes back with anything, which I hope and expect she'll do. I'll get straight back to you if she does.

'Anyway, my bill at the Sofitel for this trip's already so high they'd probably need more authorisation from the Police Commissioner if I stay here any longer. But thanks for the experience anyway. They have a particularly good brand of caviar here.'

'You'll keep, mate….'

* * *

The outback may be isolated in some ways, but it only took me a day to get back from Melbourne to Coen. One plane from Melbourne to Cairns, and the Bushpilots' plane from Cairns to Coen in the evening. That plane then sits at Coen overnight, ready for the flight back to Cairns at six the next morning. My vehicle was still at Coen Airport, and I got a nice welcome from Stuey when I got back to the pub. I think I must have added a dash of extra colour up there, because he shouted me a beer when I arrived. Maybe I was his best source of income at the moment – there still didn't seem to be many people staying at the pub.

Next morning I was unpacking and reorganising after Melbourne when Elsie arrived to clean. She came in and closed the door, then said: 'You know that thing you asked me the other day. I got on to my aunties, and they just got back to me. There's an airstrip a bit past what you fellers call Bramwell Station. It's a bit north of here – that's why it took 'em a bit of time to find out what's goin' on. A little plane comes in there, always of a Wednesday morning, and there's someone in a ute that meets it. They get packages off of the plane and the ute takes 'em away. My aunties didn't know where the plane comes from, but they think it's the same plane and the same ute. Most of the time, anyway.'

'Thanks, Elsie, that's great. I should know where Bramwell Station is, but I can't remember.'

'It's a bit of a way up. You take the main road out of Coen to the airport. Past the airport, past the Archer River, and then there's the old telegraph road. You go along that past Wenlock, and past an old airstrip. Then a bit of a way further the road turns right to Bamaga. You go along that, past Bramwell Station, and a bit further up you go left. You can't miss it – it's the only road turning off that way. A bit of a way down there you'll find the airstrip. There's another station near it, but I don't know the whitefeller name for that one. The road that goes up to the strip's not real good. That's what my aunties told me, anyway.'

'Thank you, Elsie – that's a huge help. I hope that'll help us to stop this trade in drugs, which'll help your people as well.

I should check if there's a reward for information like that. Sometimes there is when it's about solving crimes.'

'If there's anything like that, you please give it to the school. If you give it direct to people, with some of 'em it'll go on the grog. Another problem we gotta solve.' She turned and grinned at me. 'Maybe you could give it to the school to help one of our young girls go to uni. She could study your insects. I always thought that sounded like something interesting, after them other fellers was here.'

'Point taken, Elsie, and that's a very good idea about the uni. And you're right about the insects. I reckon I'm very lucky to have a chance to work with them. I'll see what I can do. No promises, but I'll try.'

Then I had one further thought. 'Elsie, you said that the plane always comes on a Wednesday morning. Would there be any reason for that, do you know?'

'I dunno for sure, but my aunties did say there's a station a bit away from the airstrip. Most of the stations I know, the people there go shopping on one particular day in the week. Maybe that mob always goes on a Wednesday. Then they wouldn't hear the plane coming in, or see anything. Only the blackfellers'd see it,' she added with a wink.

* * *

Immediately after Elsie had done the room I called Alan Campbell to pass on this latest information. Needless to say, he was delighted.

'I'll get straight on to Dave Schiller and Merv Tansley. That'll give us all a firmer basis for planning some real surveillance.

We've got some trackers installed on vehicles now, but this'll give us a specific site at which to monitor plane arrivals, and vehicles meeting the planes. Thanks, mate – you're finally worth all the money!'

That was high praise from Alan....

ALAN CAMPBELL

Dave, Merv and I met to discuss the new development. Merv went first.

'We've been monitoring the tracker that we put under Wayne Robertson's ute, and we've logged his pattern of movements over the last week. So far it hasn't led to anything exciting, but it's working well. No dropouts yet, anyway. He's visited several properties and a couple of meatworks. Could be to do with dodgy meat, or it could all be quite legit. Time will tell.

'We've also got three of Ioannides' long-haul trucks with trackers, and we might try and do a fourth. They've been doing the regular runs up and down the east coast. They've mostly been going between a meatworks and Ioannides' factory, but after loading meat one of them's also called at another warehouse before returning to Melbourne. It could be where a dummy fuel tank with drugs was then fitted, but we don't want to move at this stage. We'd much rather build up a substantial pattern before we move in. If we've misjudged anything at this stage we'll blow the whole lot.

'Another thing that's happening is that the driver of the truck that had the bodies in it is being released. It was technically an offence to carry the human bodies, and proceedings will follow – most likely against the Ioannides company rather than the driver. Given that there was no crime involved with the bodies, like murder or something, we've been given permission to make it all low key so that Ioannides doesn't think that there's any serious surveillance still going on.

'And the final thing that'll be done is the installation of some sort of surveillance at that airstrip that Gil was told about. We're still working on that at the moment. The directions weren't the most precise, but we reckon we've identified which one Elsie meant. We don't want anything obvious because that might frighten off anyone collecting shipments there. We had been thinking of something like a dummy communications repeater, but the aerial shots of the airstrip that I've so far been able to find show that it's pretty bare around there. If a new mast with a gizmo on it suddenly appeared, it'd probably arouse suspicion. We think there may be a small stand of trees just beyond the western end of the strip, however, and we might then be able to fasten something to one of the trees that wouldn't be spotted. I'm going up there tomorrow with one of our surveillance experts, and we'll see what we can sort out.'

GIL REYNOLDS

I'd broadened my survey to include all blowflies and flies of veterinary importance in the Cape York Peninsula area, while at the same time hoping to find the adult fly that relates to Anna's maggots. The work was going faster because I'd got a permanent base at the hotel instead of trying to do it while camping, and my boss had permitted me to stay on longer at the hotel. I suspect he did a deal with Stuey, but that was between him and Stuey.

Late one afternoon, as I was just pinning and labelling the last flies for the day, there was a tap at the door. I went to the door and found Elsie. She looked slightly apprehensive, so I invited her to come in.

'How's it all going, Elsie. Done for the day?'

'Yeah, I'm off in a few minutes.' She paused for a moment. 'I was just going to ask you....' She stopped again, then said: 'My folks said they wouldn't mind meeting you. They was wondering if you'd like to come up their way, maybe Saturday?'

I certainly hadn't expected that, and I was a bit gob-smacked. 'Jeez, Elsie, that's very kind of them. I don't know that I'm a very interesting sort of guy, but I'd love to meet your folks. I'd be very privileged to do so.'

'That's good, I'll tell 'em tonight.'

'How would I know how to get to them?'

'Bit difficult to explain. Best might be if I came with you in your truck, after I knock off on Saturday. If you don't mind me riding with you, of course.'

'Elsie, I'd love it. You can introduce me to your country as we go, as well as to your people.'

Elsie looked very pleased and wished me good night as she left. A bit later I went down to the bar for a beer, and I told Stuey about the invite.

'Jeez, mate, you must be really well in with Elsie. I've been up there myself because I'm almost part of the family now, but I've never heard her invite anyone else before. You'll be in for an interesting evening. Long one, too. You got a swag with you?'

'Yeah, I always carry one if I'm going bush. Even when I'm actually staying at a five-star pub like this one.'

Stuey grinned. 'That's good, mate, because it'll be a long evening, and you'll probably want to doss down there at the end of it. Not good to try and drive back again afterwards. Too many animals on the road, and there'll be a bit of grog as well.'

Gulp...

* * *

On the Saturday evening Elsie and I set off in my wagon. We went north and then east from Coen, and finished up with a few wiggles of tracks. I could see why Elsie'd said that I mightn't find the way myself. No doubt about it.

We arrived at a smallish settlement of simple houses, and there were already some people assembled round a large central fire. Elsie pointed me to an area a bit away from the gathering.

'You can park here, mate. You won't be in nobody's way here.'

Before we got out of the vehicle she told me what to expect, mainly so that I didn't embarrass anyone with inappropriate actions, I guessed. Then she took me over to the group and sat me down. Luckily I'm still just flexible enough to sit cross-legged, because there weren't any seats of any sort. She'd told me not to try to talk to anyone until the main person to perform the welcome came out.

After a few minutes an elderly man with a magnificent flowing beard came out. He sat opposite me and spoke very solemnly, entirely in his language. Then a broad, shallow dish containing smoking leaves was brought out and placed in front of the elder. He continued to speak.

Eventually he stopped speaking, and Elsie gave me a gentle nudge. She'd told me that at that point I should respond, so I said:

'I acknowledge you as the traditional owners and custodians of this land, and I respect your good stewardship of the land, the waters and the seas around you. I thank you for this warm welcome to your land.'

My words were translated by a man sitting next to the elder as I spoke, and the elder seemed to be pleased. As far as I could make out, anyway – there wasn't much expression on his rather still face. Then the remaining members of the group all joined in with what I thought must have been their own less formal welcome.

Some drink was brought out in a wooden container. It was offered first to the elder, and then to me. I've no idea what it was, but it was quite pleasant and refreshing. After I'd drunk some it was passed around the rest of the group, and then the formality seemed to be over. Beer was brought out for those who wanted it, and some small floury cakes with a nicely savoury taste. Several of the group had come over to sit closer to me, and I asked them what the cakes were.

They told me their name for them, which I couldn't pick up fully, and then said: 'Bush tucker, mate. Grass that grows around here. We get the seeds off of it and the women grind it up into flour and bake it. Good tucker, eh?' And it certainly was.

Some of the men who spoke good English asked me about the work I was doing up in their land, and they seemed both pleased and interested. They asked some pretty smart questions, too. They asked me if the screwworms would attack the Australian tree kangaroos and wallabies if they ever got in from PNG, and I had to admit that I was stumped on that one. I told them I'd try to find out from some people in PNG whether they'd ever noticed that, since those animals are found in PNG as well.

After a beer or two more and some more chat, some of the men went over to a spot on the ground where smoke was coming out, and opened the top. It revealed itself to be an oven dug into the ground, and after a bit of shuffling various cooked foods were brought out and arranged on wooden trays. These were offered first to the old elder, and next to me. There were several meats, some fish and shellfish, and a number of vegetables, and I chose some bits to put on a wooden platter that I'd been given. Somebody else brought a tray of raw fruits, and I picked some of those as well. I hoped I hadn't infringed any protocols with what I was doing. I figured that Elsie, who was hovering, would have given me a nudge if I did something wrong.

The platters were then put down and everybody hoed in. Relative silence descended as people ate, and while we were munching I noticed a youngish girl who was watching me quite closely. However, I was chatting to the guy next to me about the food.

'What sort of meat would this one be?'

'Him? That's kangaroo tail. Good tucker. When it's well cooked like this, it just falls off the bone. We was going to get some crocodile for you, but we couldn't get none. That's real good tucker, that is.'

'And this one?'

'That's a native bird you get in the forest.'

'Cassowary?'

'Nah, the cassowary's our totem, so we don't eat them.'

'And these fruits?'

'Don't know your names for them, mate – sorry.'

It didn't matter too much – I was just enjoying trying them all. I'd ask Elsie later if she knew the names of some of them, or even Stuey might.

The young girl had still been watching me and finally she came over, a bit tentatively.

'Hello, mister.'

'Hi there. What's your name?'

'I'm Millie. You're the man who studies the flies on the cattle, are you?'

'That's right, I am. Do you know about them, then?'

'Elsie told me about you. She's my auntie.' She paused, obviously trying to decide whether to say more. 'I was wondering' – more pause – 'whether I could come and have a look at your work some time?'

'Millie, you'd be really welcome if your family doesn't mind. Are you specially interested in insects then?'

'Mister, I love going out on country. The elders have taken me out a bit and told me some of the stories about our country, but I know you fellers also know a lot of things about the animals and the plants, and I'd love to learn more.' She paused again. 'I wouldn't mind going to university one day. But I guess it costs a lot of money, doesn't it?'

'Yeah, I'm afraid it does, but there are also some ways you can get it paid for you. My pa and ma didn't have much money but I was able to get a scholarship for uni which paid a lot of the cost. You might be able to do the same. Anyway, if you'd like to come and see my work I'd be very happy to show it to you, and we can probably get Elsie to organise it. And by the way, I'm not mister – I'm just Gil.' I grinned to soften the comment.

She gave me a long look, then said: 'Thanks – Gil!' – and she went off to talk to Elsie.

I chatted on for a while with some of the guys, while beers appeared at intervals and remnants of food were circulated. Eventually the elder who'd greeted me got up, came over to me and bade me goodnight, and I thanked him for so warmly welcoming me to his country. Then Elsie came over with a man who she said was one of her brothers. She said I could unroll my swag at his place, so I collected it from my wagon and he showed me where. It seemed at that stage that most people were calling it a night, so I did the same.

In the morning there was tea and some baked flour cakes, and then Elsie and I were off back to Coen.

On the way back I mentioned to her about Millie's request to see more of my work. It didn't seem to come as a surprise to her, and I was fairly sure that she would have put Millie up to it. It also crossed my mind that Millie might have been the girl she was thinking about with her question about people going to university. Elsie didn't waste time when she got an idea.

Elsie said: 'She's a good girl, Millie. Bright, too. I'm hoping she can finish at school well, and maybe go to a college. Any suggestions you can make for her, I know she'd be real glad.'

'If she wants to see my work I'd suggest that we go first to Ray Smith's place. You know I've got some cages for rearing flies in one of his sheds?'

'Yeah, my cousin told me.' The bush network was in good working order.

'Then we could go to the pub and I'll show her the rest of the work. But are you sure you're happy about me doing this – you know, a young girl and an older man. I don't know what your people might think about that.'

Elsie gave me a long look. 'I reckon you're okay, and I'll tell 'em that. Anyway, if there's any problem at Ray's me cousin Chaz is there to sort it out, and if there's any problem at the pub I'll beat the daylights out of yer!' She was grinning as she said it.

ALAN CAMPBELL

Merv Tansley, who was looking after the drugs side of our investigation, had gone to north Queensland to look at the airstrip where Elsie's family had said a plane lands at intervals and unloads something. He'd taken a surveillance technician with him, and they'd flown to Cairns and hired a four-wheel drive from the airport. There was to be no contact with local police, to maintain complete security.

There wasn't a lot that we could do in the meantime, so Dave Schiller of the stock squad told me a bit more about cattle theft in Queensland.

'Mate, I think you're already aware that cattle duffing's pretty widespread in the state. Well, not just us, actually – the other Aussie states have pretty much the same problems.

'One of the problems we all face is that it's bloody hard to get any evidence that'll stand up in court. You take a grazier who drives some cattle off a neighbour's property into his own. It's usually unbranded calves because they're harder to identify, but they'll take branded cattle as well. If the beasts are found there the cocky just says the boundary fence must have broken and the cattle strayed in. If they're in a pen he says he'd rounded them up so he could return 'em to the owner. You can't prove it isn't true.'

'That's pretty much of a mongrel act to pinch your neighbour's cattle.'

'Yeah, well, you'd be surprised at how often that happens. Price of livestock these days, it's pretty lucrative, and a lot less work for the money. As far as we know the majority of the duffing is small scale local. There are a number of bigger professionals, though. One or two have even got trucks rigged out as mobile abattoirs, though trucks like that are also harder to conceal. More of them have smaller trucks that can take livestock in the back, or they tow a livestock trailer. Then they take the beasts to a small abattoir – sometimes an illegal one – and they're butchered there.

'The real big professionals are smart. They do most of their raids on nights of full moon, when they won't have to use headlights and attract attention to their vehicles. They even de-bark their dogs so they don't make any noise while they're rounding up animals.'

'Isn't there any foolproof system of marking animals, so their origin can always be seen?'

'There are various ways, but the "foolproof" bit's the catch. The initial legislation said that all beasts had to have either an ear tag or a tail tag. The trouble with that is that tags can easily be cut off. Then there's ear-marking, where you have a notch or notches cut out of an ear at a specific point. But those can be cut away as well. Then there's branding – either by freezing, or hot irons, or by electric branding. It's a bit better, but other brands can then be applied afterwards and they largely obscure the initial ones.

'One smarter way that's come up more recently is a small radio device. It's a microchip transmitter that can be put either in an ear tag or in a small pellet that's deposited internally into the animal's rumen. The snag with that's been that some grazier's don't want to pay out for those – they're about seven dollars per device, which for a herd amounts to quite a bit. It's a rather false economy when the beast itself may be worth a grand, but that's what happens.'

'Geez, mate, I thought I had a tough job but I wouldn't swap it for yours, that's for sure.'

* * *

When Merv Tansley got back from the airstrip he called the three of us together.

'Hi guys, I thought I'd better update you on how it went up north. As you know I went up with Viktor Karlsson, who's one of our best surveillance people and absolutely trustworthy.

'We spent a bit of time identifying the particular airstrip from Elsie's directions, but in the end I'm sure we've got the right one. And Elsie was right when she said that the last bit of road wasn't real flash. We made sure that we didn't get there on the Wednesday, just in case the plane came in that day.

'We did a good recce of the airstrip and its surrounds. It's in quite good nick considering that the property that's about a kilometre away doesn't seem to use it, though I suppose they could get supplies or something delivered there by someone else. And looking at the dirt surface of the runway there could have been faint tyre marks on it, though it's a pretty hard surface and we couldn't really tell.

The strip does have trees just past its western end, and a surveillance gadget mounted on one of them would give a good view of anything landing on the strip.

'Viktor had brought several bits of kit with him, and he was able to set up a recording camera on one of the trees and a solar panel higher up to ensure its power supply. When he'd got it mounted we both went back and peered at where we knew it was, and you absolutely couldn't see it even when you knew the spot exactly.

'Then we thought we'd go and check out the people in the station homestead that's not far away. When we got there an elderly lady was hanging washing on a line. We went up to her and said we were from the Department of Civil Aviation and were following up a report of a missing plane – had she heard any around the property about last Wednesday? She said no, she and her husband went every Wednesday to shop in Coen, and they usually didn't get back till about four o'clock. Then she called into the house and her husband came out, and he said the same. He was also pretty old, and we noted that both seemed to be rather deaf.

'There were presumably some stockmen around, though we didn't see any. If there were, some of them might have been from Elsie's mob, but most people wouldn't bother asking them.'

'So where do we go from here, Merv?'

'We wait for Wednesday and see if anything comes up. I don't imagine that they come every Wednesday, but Viktor's set the gizmo up so that it'll send a signal if it picks up anything substantial, and we can retrieve its memory remotely. God knows how he does it, but that's what he says. We'll see, won't we?'

GIL REYNOLDS

Elsie suggested that if I was still prepared to show Millie my work, she could come to Coen on the coming Saturday when she wouldn't be at school. Elsie said one of her cousins (of whom there seemed to be multiple) could bring her to Pascoe Downs, where I'd meet her and show her what I was doing there. We could go out round the traps in the forest at Pascoe, and inspect the rearing facilities in the shed near the homestead. Then I'd bring her to Coen and show her the lab set-up in my hotel room, and Elsie would take her back home at the end.

Saturday came, and when I got to Pascoe Downs I found Millie already there and chatting to Elsie's cousin Chaz. The three of us talked together for a few minutes, then Chaz excused himself to go and clean some gear.

I took Millie to the shed where my rearing cages were spread around the benches. I pointedly left the door open so just in case anyone might have wondered what we were doing in there. After all, they didn't yet know me all that well up this way.

'So this is where I rear my samples to become adult flies. Sorry about the smell – it gets pretty high in here.'

'No worse than you get out on country when you find a dead animal. Doesn't worry me much.'

'I've come with a drawing of the different stages in the life of a fly. I thought it might help to explain what I'm actually doing, but I'm not a good artist so it may not help all that much.

'Anyway, here's an adult fly. The female fly develops eggs inside her body – anything from fifteen or twenty up to fifty or more – depends on which fly we're talking about. She lays the eggs on to whatever the fly's going to breed in – in our case it's dead meat. She pokes them into the surface of the meat, and the eggs lie there for a day or so. Then they hatch into what we call a larva, though most people would call it a maggot.

'The maggots have three stages – a tiny one, which has very few features for telling which type of fly it is, then a second stage which has a few more features but still not many, and finally a third stage which has all the features that you need to work out which fly it is. All the while the maggot's busily feeding on the dead meat, which is how it grows.

'Then the larva goes quiet, and turns into what's called a pupa. That's this rather blobby looking thing in the picture. It consists of the outside skin of the last stage larva, and that skin becomes a hard and tough shell. Inside that shell the rest of the larva turns into an adult fly. When it's finished the body of the fly is well-developed, but the wings are folded up and look rather scrunched. When the new fly feels it's ready to go, it splits open the shell of the pupa and comes out. It sits still for a short while as everything hardens off, and at the same time it blows up its wings and stretches them out. Finally it's ready to go, and it flies away to feed. It has to feed for a few days before it's had enough food to develop its first batch of eggs, and at that point we're back where we started on this picture. Does any of that make sense to you?' I grinned at her so that it didn't sound too much like a test.

'Yeah, I reckon that's pretty clear. Do you have any of those stages here that I could have a look at?'

'I should be able to do all of them except maybe the eggs, though we can look for those too. It just depends whether any of my flies have laid any within the last day or so – otherwise they'll have hatched.

'Anyway, inside these cages along this bench there are adult flies. There's blue ones, green ones, dull brown ones, grey ones, and in this cage here is my prize find – they're an orange colour.'

'Yeah, I think I know them. You can find them sometimes in our forests when you find a dead pig, or something that a pig's killed. There's two sorts – a big one and a small one.'

'That's very interesting, because I've only found the one sort – this one. Is this the big one or the small one?'

'I reckon this is the small one. You don't find the big one as often, but it's sometimes there. It's brighter orange than this one.'

'Wow. I'd love to come out with you some time and we could try to catch the big orange one. I'm supposed to study every single type of fly up here, and that'd be a rare and good one.'

'Yeah, I'd be happy to try that. You don't know when you're going to see them, but it might be worth a go.'

I could be getting a valuable new field assistant here....

'Right, these cages along here are supposed to have the larvae or maggots in the meat, and I've taken the adult flies out of them. Let's have a look at the samples.'

I pulled out a dish of meat, and a quick poke showed that it was heaving with maggots. I watched Millie to see if she recoiled, but she was peering closely with great interest.

'I reckon these'd be the second stage of the maggots, with about half the features developed. The first stages are even smaller – just tiny white specks that wriggle. Now I'll show you the older maggots that are nearly fully developed.'

I pulled out another tray that had large and very mobile maggots in the meat.

'And now for the pupa, if I can find any.'

I got out another tray in which the meat was a bit more dried up and shrivelled, and I carefully lifted up the piece of meat. There was nothing immediately underneath, but when I poked gently through the sand on which it had been lying I revealed a number of quite large pupae, darkish brown in colour.

'So that's what the pupa looks like. Now I'll try to find an empty one from which the adult fly's already come out.'

I looked down the cages until I spotted something very lucky.

'Come over here and I'll show you something that you don't see very often. Those two flies hanging on the wire at the back of the cage – can you see that they look very pale and their wings don't look like proper fly wings? They're rather scrunched up. Those flies have only just come out of the pupa, and they're still hardening off.'

'Wow, I've never seen that before.' She looked quite enthusiastic, and I sensed that living things fascinated her.

'I won't look for an empty pupa in there even though they'd be there, because I'd disturb the flies when they're delicate.

I'll have a look in this one. I pulled out yet another dish and dug around in the sand, and came up with half a dozen empty pupae.

'Pick it up and have a look at it. See how it's quite crisp and hard, and it's completely empty inside. Not long ago there was one of those flies squashed inside it. Amazing, isn't it?'

'Jeez, this is really interesting. I'd love to study something like this when I'm grown up.'

'Well, maybe you will be able to. But we haven't quite finished yet because I said I'd try to find you some eggs.'

I pulled out a tray from a cage where I hadn't long put the meat in with the flies, and when I poked gently under the surface of the meat I found a batch of twenty or so long, thin cylindrical objects, glistening white.

'Those are the eggs. As I said, they'll sit like that for about a day, maybe a bit longer, and then each one'll split open. They have a line like a seam down the long side, and that splits open and the tiny first stage maggot wriggles out and gets stuck straight into its tucker – the meat.'

And since she was showing so much interest in all of this, I thought I'd add one more interesting fact.

'Now you've seen all the stages of a fly's life, but there's one difference with a few types of flies. Every insect in the world has some sorts of enemies. Dragonflies, some other types of flies, and some other insects try to catch the adult flies, but the adult flies are usually able to fly away and escape.

'Other things like beetles root around in dead meat trying to find and eat the fly maggots, but the maggots can wriggle away very fast and most of them escape. The pupae can't move, but they're buried pretty well in the soil under the meat and they're pretty hard and difficult for other insects to break into. Some might be found by their enemies, but most'd be pretty safe. The one stage that isn't safe is the egg. As you saw, it's only just under the surface of the meat, and some things, beetles particularly, are very good at finding them. So some flies have thought up a way to get around that. Any ideas on how they might do that?'

Millie looked at me for a while, then slowly shook her head.

'Don't worry, I never knew this either until my uni lecturer told me about it. The mother fly develops a batch of eggs, but she doesn't lay them in anything – she holds them inside her body while they develop. Then when the tiny maggots have hatched out inside her, she lays the moving maggots directly on top of the meat and they immediately wriggle into the meat so they can escape any enemies. So you never see the egg stage of those flies – they're only ever inside the mother.'

'Hey, that's really neat. Thank you so much for telling me all this, and for showing me.'

'No worries at all. I just love it that somebody else is interested in these things. Most people I meet just say "Yuk!" and don't want to hear any more. Anyway, there's one more thing to show you, back at the hotel. After that Elsie'll get you back to your family.'

We drove back to Coen, said hi to Stuey on the way in and then went to look for Elsie. We found her in the kitchen.

'Hi, Elsie. I've brought my new assistant to meet you.'

She grinned. 'Hello, Millie. How's it all going?'

'It's really cool, Auntie. I know a lot more about flies than I did before. And maggots!'

'Hm, Gil must be a good teacher to get a reaction like that.'

I said: 'We're just going to look at the pinned flies in my room, and after that Millie's all yours.'

We went to my room, and once again I made sure to leave the door open.

'Right, first thing. Have you ever seen one of these before?'

She shook her head.

'It's a microscope. You put a fly or a maggot under here and look down these eyepieces here. It makes what's underneath really big so you can see all the details. I'll get one of my pinned flies and you can have a look.'

I put a large blue blowfly under the microscope and showed Millie how to adjust the width of the eyepieces and then focus.

She set them and then gasped. 'I've never seen anything like this. It's like magic!'

'Can you see the things like thick hairs or bristles all over the fly?'

'Yeah, there's lots of them on this one.'

'They're very important for telling exactly which fly this is. The numbers and patterns vary between the different types of flies, but they're always the same for one type.'

I showed her my boxes of pinned flies of the various colours, including the orange one, and she said it was definitely the small species. Finally I showed her a male and a female of one species, and pointed out how you could tell between the sexes.

'See this one? It's got two huge eyes at the front that just about join together. That's the male. He needs to have huge eyes so that he can find a female fly easily when he's flying around. This one's the female. Her eyes are still quite big, but they're not as big as the male and there's a gap between the two eyes.

'And that's about all I can tell you. Now you know almost

as much as I do about flies, and a lot more than most people!'

'It's fantastic, Gil. Thanks a million. I'd really like to do something like this when I'm grown up.'

'Well, I reckon you've got a good eye for it. The one thing we've still got to do some time is go hunting in the forest. I can show you how I try to find as many flies in the bush as I can, and you can show me what you know about your country and what lives in it. And maybe we'll find the big and bright orange fly, too.'

ALAN CAMPBELL

Dave Schiller and I didn't hear from Merv Tansley for nearly two weeks. Then he called us both in for a meeting.

'I'd like to be giving you some positive news, but there isn't much to report yet. The good news is that the surveillance thingy that Viktor set up at the airstrip is working. It set off a signal and sent a picture a few days ago when a cow wandered along the airstrip. Good picture of a Braford heifer, but not directly relevant to our enquiries.

'Last Wednesday came and went, and no plane came in. We always thought that it wouldn't be every week, and we presume that the gizmo would have picked it up since it scored the cow, but it's still frustrating when you're waiting for something to happen. We'll see what happens this coming Wednesday. If still nothing, then we thought that maybe we'd ask Gil Reynolds to drive up there and motor from one end of the airstrip to the other and we can check that we pick him up and how well. Alan, do you think that could be organised?'

'I'm sure there wouldn't be any problem. He'd be pretty

flexible with his time with the sort of work he does, and he might welcome the chance to collect flies in that part of the world. It's a bit further north than most of what he's done, and northwards is good. You'd have to think exactly how much you'd tell him about what and why before we ask him. I don't think he knows all of what's been done up there, and it's probably best if it stays that way.'

'Yeah, good point. And now I have to give you the bad news. We've stopped receiving anything from the tracker on Wayne Robertson's truck. We don't know whether it's run out of juice, but those things usually last for close to forever, or whether it's simply dropped off or been knocked off accidentally. They usually stick well, but it could happen.

'But the real worry is that it may have happened because he's discovered it and removed it himself. In that case it would mean that he's got wise to the fact that he's under surveillance for something or other. He wouldn't necessarily think it's because of the drugs – he might think dodgy cattle movements – but either way it's going to make it much harder to follow him. The only thing we can think of at the moment is to place another one on the truck, in a spot where it'd be very hard to discover it, but it could be tricky to get a chance to do that surreptitiously. I think we're going to have to try, though.

'What we're doing at the moment is some on-the-ground surveillance just to watch what he does and where he goes, to see if there's any sign of increased awareness and carefulness about movements and so on. So far it doesn't look like it and we may be lucky, but we're going to have to be very careful about what we do and how.'

'Okay, Merv, thanks for that. Tough, I can see. Let us know what you'd like Gil to do if no plane comes in on Wednesday, and we'll organise it. Otherwise, best of luck with the rest of it.'

GIL REYNOLDS

I'd agreed with Elsie that once more at a weekend I'd take her to her folk, and then pick up Millie to go fly-hunting in the forest. I packed an insect net, some tubes for getting the flies out of the net when I'd caught them, and a couple of light cages with some sugar and water soaked on to cotton wool. We drove via Pascoe Downs so that I could also pick up some stinking meat for bait. Fresh meat from Coen wouldn't have attracted anything for at least a couple of days.

I had no idea where to go from Pascoe Downs, so Millie was my guide. We drove to a large patch of forest where Millie said she'd seen the large, bright orange fly, which I was fairly sure must be another blowfly. It seemed as good a place as any to start.

We stopped at a clearing just inside the thicker vegetation, and Millie led me along a barely discernible track.

'You stop wherever you want, Gil. I'm just the watcher on this.'

'Millie, I think you'll be a lot more than that. Let's do this together. And you can go first because you know where you're going.'

We walked quietly along the faint track. Once Millie stopped at a shrub bearing some small, bright red fruits, a bit like cherries.

'Good tucker, this one. Healthy too. I don't know the white man's name for this one, but it's real nice.'

We walked on a bit, and then I said to Millie: 'Can we stop here and put some bait out? We're well into the forest, and this looks like a good spot.'

I unpacked my net and tubes, then got out the stinking meat and dug out a chunk. I put it on the ground and we waited. It wasn't long before flies started coming to it, but they were all ones that I'd already collected. I took the opportunity to show Millie how to use an insect net to catch the flies without fouling the net with the bait, and it didn't take her long to get the knack.

Then she saw a flash of orange buzzing round, and eventually the fly settled. Millie said: 'That's not the one I wanted to show you. That's the little one.'

'I might still catch it, though. I haven't got many samples of this one and I'll take it back to Pascoe Downs to set up a colony.'

That done we moved on further into the forest. Suddenly Millie turned round to me and put her finger to her lips. Then she very slowly and quietly crept forward, beckoning me with her. A little way ahead we saw a large bird which I recognised as a cassowary, emu-sized, with blue and red on its long neck and the characteristic tall, curved casque on its head. I'd seen them in captivity before, but it was the first time I'd ever seen one in the wild. However, even better were the two smaller birds with it – quite young cassowary chicks, with orangey fluff on their heads and longitudinal stripes down the back, alternating dark brown and very pale. I'd never seen them before except in photos.

We watched them for a short while and then the adult must have sensed us somehow because it suddenly moved off fast along the path, the two chicks trailing behind it. When they'd gone I asked Millie how she knew they were there.

'I heard them. I've come across them before, and I know the sounds.'

I didn't like to say that I'd heard absolutely nothing.

We continued along the track and Millie stopped once more, this time to collect several large greyish-brown fungi that were growing a bit off the track. She stowed them away in a small woven bag that she'd been carrying.

'Mate, this is more good tucker. My mum'll be really pleased when I come back with these.'

Once again I would have had to admit that I hadn't even noticed them. And I thought I was a reasonable field biologist….

We made one more stop along the track and put out more bait, and this time we were rewarded. Millie was particularly pleased because she might have been wondering whether I believed in her large and bright orange blowfly, but there it was. It was a male that had obviously just stopped by for a feed, but I still netted it because I didn't think it was represented in any collections. We waited a bit longer, and a female arrived, which I also caught, and then a second female. With those two I ought to be able to get eggs and then larval stages. A fantastic result.

We called it a day then and went back to the truck. As we

drove back I asked Millie if she had any books about insects, and she shook her head.

'You can't get that sort of thing up here.'

'What about your school? Do they have any books like that?'

'Nah, they don't have many books of any sort, really. Teacher's pretty good and does her best, but we haven't got much.'

'I've got to go to Brisbane soon to get some more supplies. I'll see if I can look out anything while I'm there.'

'Gee, that'd be fantastic. After what you showed me I'm busting to learn more about it all.'

* * *

Next Monday when Elsie came to do my room I said to her: 'Millie told me the other day that her school – your school – doesn't have all that many books, including on things like insects. I was wondering whether next time I was up that way I might call in at the school and see what they do have? But I wouldn't want to make it sound as though I was insulting the school or the teacher or anything. It's just that I have to go to Brisbane soon to get some more of my supplies, and I know someone there who runs an organisation that provides books and things for anything to do with teaching children. I could see if they might have anything that could help.'

'Mate, don't you worry about insulting anything or anyone. I reckon the teacher'd be only too pleased for any help she can get. She's a good lass and she does her best, but she is a bit short on some things. I could take you to her next weekend if you like.'

'That'd be great. I was planning to go to Brisbane early next week – it'd fit well.'

* * *

I was duly taken to Elsie's people's school, where I met Julie, who was indeed a young teacher. She told me she'd been out of teachers' college for a year, and was still feeling her way. However, she'd created a lively classroom atmosphere, with lots of pictures on the walls obviously done by the kids. I was impressed that a lot were of animals and plants, and there must have been a budding entomologist among them because there was a pretty good picture of a bee – even accurate down to the veins on the wings.

Julie told me she'd had to learn the local language as well as how to teach, because she came from near Normanton in the Gulf Country.

'I'm one of the Kurtijar people, so I've had to learn the Kaantju words. I get as much teaching as I give – maybe more!' She chuckled.

'So tell me what you'd like most at this school that you haven't got at the moment?'

She thought for a moment or two. 'I guess more books. What you can see in front of you's about it. I'd love some books about animals and plants. You can see from what's on the walls that the kids love that. Maybe something on aboriginal history too, if you can find any. One of the things I loved about teachers' college was that there was a library. I do miss that up here.'

'Elsie probably told you that I'm going to Brisbane on Monday, and I know someone who collects books for kids of all ages. I'll see if she can come up with anything. In the meantime good luck with everything here. It looks to me as if you're doing a pretty good job with the kids!'

ALAN CAMPBELL

The next Wednesday was approaching when a totally unexpected event upset the whole schedule.

In the absence of a tracking device on Wayne Robertson's wagon Merv Tansley had taken to doing old fashioned surveillance by discreet following with unmarked police cars. The team following Wayne rotated fairly frequently so that he wouldn't be likely to spot a tail, and because suitable personnel were a bit short Merv and I shared the load, with some staff contributed by each of us.

In a real stroke of luck, it was one of my guys who made the phone call.

'G'day, Alan – it's John Hegarty here. I've been following Wayne Robertson down the Bruce Highway, and his vehicle's just been involved in a fairly major prang a bit south of Proserpine. The front of his wagon was hit by a semitrailer. I reckon the driver of the semi might have dozed off and crossed over the middle of the road. It struck the front right side of Wayne's vehicle. Wayne's truck's still upright but quite badly damaged at the front, and I reckon Wayne's got serious chest injuries. Silly bugger didn't seem to have had his seat belt on, and I reckon he slammed into the steering wheel. The semi skewed all over the road and then overturned, and there's a hell of a mess everywhere.

'We've called for ambulances and traffic controllers but they aren't here yet. I dunno what condition the semi driver's in – I think he's alive, but I can't say any more than that yet. In view of the importance of the target I thought I'd better report this straight away to you.'

'Thanks, John – that sounds pretty bloody awful. What you've done is fine, but there's one more thing I'd like to ask you to do, and it's very important. Really, really important. You may or may not know that Wayne's suspected of being involved in a murder on top of all the other things. We've got a strong suspicion that there'll be forensic evidence in the tray of his truck, and also on the pile of tarps that are in the back, if they're still there. You said the wagon's still upright, which I hope means that the tarps are still there. Could you go over and confirm that, and then call me back?'

John rang back a few minutes later. 'Alan, the back of the wagon hasn't suffered, and I can confirm that there's quite a pile of tarps in the back. Pretty dirty, but they're there.'

'Mate, that's great. What I'd like you to do now is keep a close eye on both the truck and tarps, and make sure that they don't get moved at all. They need to stay exactly as they are, as far as that can be done in the circumstances. What I'll do now is dispatch a police recovery truck from Mackay as fast as possible. One that can haul the wagon up on to its back platform without any interference. What I need to ask you to do is make sure that the traffic people don't take it away themselves. Tell them it's a vital bit of evidence in a serious crime case, and come the heavy if they cause you any problems. Is the vehicle blocking the highway in any way?'

'Yeah, it's taking up one of the two lanes of the highway.'

'Okay, you'll have to help them to get it off on to the verge, but don't let them do any more than that. Tell them that a police truck's coming as soon as possible, and call me so I can speak to them if there's any problem.'

I didn't know how this was all going to affect the drugs side of the investigation, but I might now be able to get some good evidence towards solving Anna Ioannides' murder.

GIL REYNOLDS

It was a pain, but I was going to have to drive to Brisbane and back, not fly. The reason was that I need to pick up a supply of KAAD, and there was no way any airline would allow me to go near it with that stuff. It's a mixture of kerosene, ethyl alcohol, glacial acetic acid and dioxane, the last of those being quite dangerous. Not that the acetic acid's much better.

KAAD's far and away the best thing for killing maggots for later examination. Most things can be pickled in straight alcohol, but if you drop a maggot into alcohol it can go on wriggling for hours on end, no doubt in agony. Maggots may look soft but they've got a very tough cuticle. But drop them into KAAD and they die instantly, and also extend to a nice straight, stretched out specimen which is perfect for further treatment and examination.

I phoned my friendly contact, Laura, at the Queensland Museum to ask her to make up some KAAD, and also to pick up a selection of brochures on various insect pests from the Department of Primary Industry. I explained how Millie was becoming a de facto assistant and how keen she was to learn more about anything living, and left her to get what she could.

Then I phoned my ex-wife Nicole in Brisbane to fix a time to drop in and see her. We don't live together any longer – she'd had trouble being married to someone who was away regularly and for long periods in the field, but we're still on good terms and we meet up every now and then. She also works for the education department as an inspector of schools, so I explained about Millie to her and she promised to get together anything she could that might help Millie's school.

* * *

The drive to Brisbane was tedious, but I was looking forward to seeing Nicole again. She was French, and delightful company. I'd often regretted having to work away so often, and wondered whether if I retired we could get together again. But the realist in me knew it wouldn't ever be likely to work.

Nicole had offered me dinner on the evening after I got to Brisbane, and she was a good cook as well as good company. After getting stores of various sorts together, including a very good selection of booklets and other bits and pieces from Laura, I went to Dan Murphy's wine store to pick up an offering for the meal with Nicole. To my great delight I found two French wines by Paul Mas, in his premium range of wines called Vignes de Nicole. How could wines with a name like Nicole fail?! I didn't know what was to be served, so I got a Viognier and a Cabernet Merlot to cover all bases.

The meal turned out to be a cassoulet, which was very kind of Nicole because I know it takes a long time to prepare and cook properly, and she would never stint on anything as important as French cuisine. And the Cab Merlot went beautifully with it.

After the meal Nicole dragged out a large box, which turned out to be filled with a variety of books on all sorts of subjects, many of which I'm sure would appeal to Millie and her teacher. She must have spent a lot of time and effort finding them all, and I don't know how she managed to do the cassoulet as well. We loaded the box into my wagon for me to take back to Coen.

I told Nicole that Millie would like to get some college education when she finishes school, and Nicole said that James Cook University in Townsville would have several courses that might be of interest to Millie and what she might want to do later.

'She'd also be not so far from her home and people in Townsville, or even in Cairns. JCU's got a campus in both, but I don't know which courses are at which campus. Brisbane's a hell of a way for someone who comes from beyond Coen.

'If there's ever a chance I wouldn't mind meeting her one day. She sounds like a girl after my own heart. And I've just had a thought as I say this. I'm going to have to go to Cairns in a couple of weeks to do some school inspections, and the department will fly me both ways. Maybe while I'm in that part of the world I could take a few days leave and come on up to Coen. I've never been that far north before. Any thoughts about that?'

'That would be fantastic if you could. Actually I'd be happy to pick you up from Cairns if you'd like. The road's not all that flash for some of the way. That's if you don't mind travelling in a four-wheel drive, that is.'

'You idiot – we used to do that a lot. Not a problem. When we get there you can just introduce me as your wife, and say

I've come to see you while I'm on leave. I could mention that I'm with the department of education in Brisbane, but not that I'm a school inspector. It would be totally unethical of me to do an inspection unannounced, and I think it might really throw the teacher. You could fill me in more on the school up there, and on Millie, while we're driving up there. Maybe even on what you're doing up there, if it's not too gruesome.'

It would be gruesome, of course, but I wasn't going to mention that while we were enjoying such a nice meal.

* * *

The drive back to Coen was even more tedious than the one down, but I consoled myself with thinking of the reactions of Millie and her teacher when I got back and handed over all the trophies. I'd also mention to Millie that Nicole might know something about courses at James Cook University, and what grants might be available to help her.

ALAN CAMPBELL

The securing of Wayne's truck and its possible evidence went perfectly, thanks to John Hegarty's good work. We got one of the good forensic technicians in to examine the tarps from the back of the wagon, and also the floor of the wagon's back tray.

We didn't hear anything for a little while, and I was beginning to fear that nothing would come out of it. However, when the technician came to report back that worry was dispelled.

'I've examined the surface of the tray and the tarpaulins very carefully, and I've found traces of human tissue and blood on both. The tray surface had smeared tissue on several parts of it, particularly where there are the metal blips standing up from the base – the ones to stop things sliding around too much. Then on the tarps, the bottom one particularly, there were a few bits of tissue adhering, and a significant number of blood stains.

'I took careful samples of all of it, and I've been able to extract reliable DNA from both areas. What I need now is the

DNA information from the body in question and I can tell you whether she was ever in that truck.

'One thing puzzled me about this material. You don't normally get chunks of tissue like I found here. Bloodstains, yes, but actual pieces of tissue? You'd get that if something or someone had been deliberately butchered on the surface, but this one didn't seem quite right for that either. The bits didn't look sliced.'

'I think that's all the more evidence that this was the body that we're interested in. We believe she was murdered somewhere up the Cape York Peninsula, dumped or shallowly buried in rainforest for a couple of days or so, and then removed again and taken to Coolabah Creek in the Gulf Country and buried there. While the body was in the rainforest it was attacked by wild pigs and had chunks gouged out of it. That damage plus the fact that the body would have been decomposing somewhat was how some bits sheared off but rather roughly.'

'Yeah, well, that would fit with what I saw. It's just that I've never seen anything like that before.'

'Always pleased to widen your education, mate.'

* * *

Assuming that when we get Anna's DNA to the forensic technician it's the same as that in the truck, it still doesn't prove that Wayne Robertson killed Anna – just that his truck had carried her. But it was pretty good odds then that he was guilty.

The truck driver who hit Wayne's wagon died in hospital from his injuries. Wayne was in hospital in Mackay with six broken ribs caused by his steering wheel, and he'd also suffered concussion. He was going to be there for a little while, and when he came out he wasn't going to know what had been investigated in the wagon. And he wouldn't know if the tarps had been thrown out in the collision or what had happened to them.

We took the opportunity to look for the tracker that had originally been fitted to the vehicle. It hadn't run out of power – it was gone. Whether he'd removed it or whether it had come off accidentally there was no way of telling. Accidental's rare but it can happen, particularly if the vehicle's driven over rough ground a lot.

* * *

I got Anna's DNA profile back to the technician as fast as I could, and he confirmed that the two lots were identical. That pretty well put the finger on Wayne as Anna's killer – he was going to have to wriggle hard to get out of that one.

That left stock thefts, illegal meat and the drugs importation as the parts of the police operation still very much open. Today was Tuesday – would there be a plane flying in tomorrow to our airstrip? Could we get lucky twice in a row?

* * *

Sadly the answer to that was no. We didn't even get the Braford heifer traversing the airstrip for one more time, and we certainly didn't get a plane coming in. I discussed it with

Merv Tansley and we agreed that I'd ask Gil to drive up there and do a run up and down the airstrip in his wagon. If the surveillance device could pick him up it was certainly going to register a plane. It would also be interesting to see if we could make out his number plate from the images. We need to be able to identify the plane that's coming in as well as the person and truck that meets it.

GIL REYNOLDS

Not long after I got back from Brisbane I had a call from Alan Campbell.

'Mate, I need your help with a small job, and I don't want to explain the background in case there's a chance that somebody's listening in. You would have large scale maps of the area north of you, wouldn't you?'

"Mate?", I thought. He must need something badly. 'Fire away, Alan. I can always say no.'

He didn't even rise to that. Must be important. 'Can you look up Bramwell Station on your maps? I know you were told where it is, but apparently it still isn't easy to find when you have the instructions. You go north up the main road from Coen to Coen Airport. Past the airport, past the Archer River to the old telegraph road. I know that's marked on the maps. You go along that road past Wenlock which I'm told you can't miss, and past an old airstrip. Ignore that one, and a bit further on a road turns right to Bamaga. There's a clear sign at that junction. Go along that Bamaga road, past Bramwell Station, and a bit further on you take a left turn. There's no sign, but

I'm told it's the only road turning left anywhere around there. Several going right, but that's the only left turn.

'Just keep going along that road about 20 k's or so, and you'll get to an airstrip that's still in working condition. Apparently it's obvious when you get there because your road goes right across one end of the strip. Drive slowly along the entire strip, do a U-turn at the end and drive slowly back again. When you've done your laps give me a ring and just say "All done".

'After that you can do whatever you like. If you think it's a good spot for catching new flies then feel free to spend more time there. If not you can just go home. I'm sorry to be so uninformative, but next time I see you I'll tell you what it's all about.'

'Okay, I should be able to leave tomorrow. I probably won't stay after it's done because various things are happening here. If it's good collecting I can always go back.'

'Mate, that's another beer we'll owe you after all this. Merv Tansley'll probably be happy to shout you….'

I sat back and thought about this. The only thing that made any sense was that they'd installed some device to watch for comings and goings at the airstrip and they wanted to test it. If that was the case I could understand why they wanted to say as little as possible about it over any airwaves.

* * *

Next day I set out for the airstrip. With my large map and Alan's comments it actually wasn't too hard to find. The airstrip was certainly obvious, and I did my laps on it as requested, then rang Alan and said: 'All done'. Alan just said 'Thanks, mate. I'll call you later and tell you whether it worked or not. Cheers'.

I looked around at the vegetation to see if it would be good for collecting flies, but it didn't look exciting. Much of it was open savanna and it was unlikely that there'd be anything there that was different from that around Coen. There were a few patches of trees – one of them at one end of the runway – but they were small and not very lush. Unlikely to be rewarding, so I drove back to Coen with no plans to return.

That evening I had another call from Alan.

'Successful, you'll be pleased to hear. One question – is the number plate of your wagon QDD 814?'

'Yup.'

'You bewdy. That's two beers now, and we might even let you trade them for one whisky. Tell you more one day'

That seemed to confirm my thoughts. They must have picked up the number plate from a camera, and if they could do that on my vehicle they should be able to identify a plane. Not to mention any wagon that came to meet the plane.

* * *

Nicole took me up on my offer to host a visit to Millie's school, and I suddenly realised that I'd have to organise some people. The first person I contacted was Elsie, who thought the visit was a great idea. As agreed with Nicole, I simply told Elsie that Nicole was my wife even though we didn't live together now, and that she worked for the Department of Education. Elsie said she'd square it with the teacher and with her community.

Then I had to sort out some details with Stuey.

'Mate, I thought you'd be sick of the sight of me by now and wanting a bit of variety, so I've invited my wife to come up here for a day or two. Should be straightforward, except that we don't live together any more so I'm not quite sure what to do about sleeping arrangements.'

'When would she be coming up?'

'She's at a meeting in Cairns at the moment. It finishes tonight. I thought I'd leave here early tomorrow and drive down, stay overnight in Cairns and bring her back the next day.'

Stuey thought for a moment. 'Your room's got a double bed, but it's also got a lot of your stuff in it. There's two other rooms that are likely to be empty when your wife's here, but neither of 'em's real flash. I guess it depends on whether your wife thinks comfort outweighs having to be close to you.' He was grinning as he said this.

'Yeah, I hadn't thought this through too well. I'll give Nicole a call when her meeting finishes this arvo, and I'll let you know.'

'No worries either way, mate. I'll look forward to meeting her. We might have to turn on a bit of proper northern hospitality in the dining room for the occasion.'

My heart sank a bit there, Nicole being a good French cook. However, it was kind of Stuey and I'd just have to brief Nicole on the way up. The hospitality would probably just mean that the steak was slightly less tough than usual, and the chips were properly drained of oil.

Back in my room I peered around, and decided I could clear enough of my gear and specimens out of the way that Nicole could stay in the room if necessary. I rang her a bit later and gave her the options. She thought for a moment, then said:

'I guess sharing your room with you'd be the better option. We did live together for quite a few years, after all.'

'You're on. I'll be down in Cairns by late afternoon tomorrow, and I'll stay at the same pub as you. If you're not doing anything else in the evening, maybe we could eat together. It'd be better than the next couple of nights at the Coen Hotel…'

* * *

The trip to Cairns was uneventful, if long, and the evening meal was very nice. The hotel had an Italian chef who certainly knew his stuff. I'd forgotten what good food was like, other than Nicole's cassoulet the other night.

We packed early the next day for Coen. I was surprised at the size of the bag that Nicole had brought for a short trip to Cairns, but when I commented she told me that she'd brought a few extra things for the school. A couple of new desks, maybe, but I thought I'd better not say that.

On the way up to Coen I had plenty of time to brief Nicole on everything – Elsie's community, the school, the teacher and where she came from, and Millie. I also told her that the local people there were Kaantju. Nicole seemed to be looking forward to the whole exercise quite enthusiastically.

When we reached the hotel I introduced her to Stuey, who seemed quite taken by her. Nicole had always had an easy way with her, and I think Stuey would have promised her anything by the end of their chat.

In my room she looked around, then said: 'I don't think this'd be a real hardship for a couple of nights…' And it wasn't.

* * *

Next morning after breakfast I introduced Nicole to Elsie. Stuey had promised to release Elsie for the day so that the three of us could go up to the school, which would be in session that day. Elsie promised me that she'd lined it all up so there'd be no problem. We loaded up a couple of quite large packages that had come out of Nicole's bag, plus the box of books that I'd brought up earlier, and we were off. At my suggestion Nicole and Elsie both sat in the back of the wagon (carefully cleaned out the evening before by me), so that they could chat more easily together. The noise of the vehicle on the rather rough road was such that I could hardly hear a word that they said.

We parked outside the school and Elsie led the way in. She knocked on the door of the main classroom and went in, then turned to Nicole and said: 'Welcome to Kaantju country.' The kids all stood up and turned to her, said something in their own language, and then started clapping.

Nicole looked at them all and said: 'Thank you for this very warm welcome. I acknowledge your ownership of this land, and I am very happy to be able to see some of it. And what a beautiful classroom you have. So much light coming in through your windows!'

It was true that the room was bathed in a very pleasant light. Then Nicole continued:

'And I didn't know that I was coming into an art gallery. All these beautiful paintings on your walls. I'd love to look at them more closely, and if the artists could each tell me about their picture that would be really good.' She said this last with an enquiring look at the teacher, who said something to the kids. The classroom then erupted as they all went over to their bit of wall.

The teacher, Julie, came up and introduced herself, and Elsie quietly left the room again. Nicole then went round all the pictures, while I stood at the back being as unobtrusive as possible. The paintings were a variety of styles and artistic qualities, but the most striking thing was that they all featured the natural world – birds, animals, fishes, and trees and other plants. Perhaps that was the brief that the kids had been given. Some were bright and a bit crude. Some were a bit impression-istic, and a few were done in very much an aboriginal style of painting – one or two extremely good. Nicole had a good word or question for each of them, and all the kids looked highly delighted by the end.

When they had finished the tour Nicole took the two packages and the box of books that I'd carried in, and gave them to Julie.

'These are a few more things that I brought from Brisbane. I didn't have everything ready when Gil came back the other day.'

Julie opened the packages, and they were full of art materials – pens, crayons, textas, pencils, paints and brushes and other assorted bits. Then there were sheets of paper of various sizes and types, and some more books, including several art books.

The kids gasped, and Julie looked a bit overwhelmed. 'You shouldn't have done so much for us,' she almost whispered.

'It's my great pleasure, and I know a source of these things in Brisbane. They're glad to provide things like this to schools that can use them. I think it's because they had good things themselves when they were at school, and they want others to have the same.'

I was fairly sure that the source would actually have been Nicole herself. I must ask her when we're back at the hotel.

Julie then said: 'Well kids, we have to get back to work now, but please give a big thanks to Miss Nicole for coming to see us all, and for bringing all these wonderful things.'

There was a rousing cheer. Then Julie said to Nicole: 'I believe I'll see you again at lunchtime?'

'Yes – I'm looking forward to it. Would you also like to ask Millie to join us after lunch?'

* * *

Lunch was a simple but very tasty affair. Some white bread that Julie said was made from native seeds, with a little meat for a topping; then some native fruits which I didn't know. Julie told us the names, but in Kaantju and I couldn't do any English versions. As we ate Nicole asked Julie if she thought Millie would be a good person to get further training at a college or university. Julie said:

'I can't think of anyone better. She's a sensible and level-headed kid, and she's very smart. She specially loves anything to do with nature – animals, plants, anything like that. She's already learnt a lot about all those things – a lot more than I ever have. She's learnt some of it by herself, just watching living things, and some of it from the Kaantju elders. I've noticed recently they even ask her about things occasionally, which is very unusual for someone her age.'

'So what we need to do now is find some way to get a grant to pay for her to go. There'll be plenty of suitable courses at James Cook University, and she wouldn't have to go as far as Brisbane if she went there. Where did you do your teacher training?'

'It was in Townsville.'

'And you got a scholarship or something?'

'A scholarship. I was very lucky.'

'Well, I think we could make a good case out for Millie too. She would have a year or two before she's old enough, but I can start making some enquiries now. The Department of Education has a special fund to help aboriginal students, and they're always on the lookout for good ones. I've been impressed already by what I've seen of Millie, and Gil speaks very highly of her too. That plus your own recommendation for her should be enough to get her some funding. Do you want to give her a wave to come over and join us?'

Millie came over, and Nicole asked her what she would most like to do in adult life. Millie thought for a moment, then said:

'I think I'd like most of all to be something like a ranger. I love our country, and it needs looking after. Our ways are not always the same as white people's ways, and we need to get more agreement between the two. I'd really like to help do that, but I'd need to learn more about the country and what's in it before anyone would be ready to listen to me.'

I was amazed at how mature a statement that was, and Nicole looked impressed too.

'Well, Gil has spoken highly of you – I think you've already been finding some good flies for him, and he's supposed to be the expert.' She flashed me a quick grin. 'When I get back to Brisbane I'll ask a few questions and see how we might be able to help. How old are you now?'

'Sixteen.'

'So it might be in two years' time that you'd be looking to start. I'll see what I can do.'

'Thank you so much, Miss Nicole.'

'Nicole's fine, thanks – otherwise I might have to call you Miss Millie!'

Millie grinned, and blushed.

It was time to take our leave of the school and the community, but Nicole asked if we could just say a proper goodbye to all the kids before we left. They were just gathering for afternoon lessons, so Nicole stuck her head inside the door and said:

'Thank you all for welcoming us to your lovely school. This seems to be one of the happiest schools I've ever been to, and I've enjoyed every minute. Good luck to you all!'

After a rousing farewell we left. I was very pleased with the way the visit had gone, though I couldn't help being a little sad that for some of the kids there wouldn't be much good luck in the future. However, I hoped we'd taken Millie a good step forward.

We found Elsie, and she again sat in the back with Nicole to discuss the day while I drove back to Coen. When we got back to the hotel we both felt that we needed a drink after the intense day, so we adjourned to the bar. They were a bit light on for French wines, but we found an acceptable Hunter Valley Semillon. As we sipped I said to Nicole:

'May I ask what you discussed with Elsie on the way there and back?'

'Secret women's business! No, not really. Elsie just gave me her take on everything. She's very perceptive, and I reckon she doesn't let much get in her way when she thinks something should be done.'

'And that comment's equally perceptive. Thank you so much for coming on this excursion. I think it meant a huge amount to the school, and it did to me too. You're an absolute natural at interacting with a wide range of people. I just sat back and admired your performance today.'

'Well, it wasn't much of a performance, really. They were all so nice it made it easy. But I hope we've helped them a bit, and maybe we can help Millie further in the future.'

We drank to that.

ALAN CAMPBELL

Before Wayne Robertson's accident, analysis of his movements when the tracker was working, and afterwards when he was being followed, showed that he had three places that he visited regularly. One was a meat processing plant, and two were companies that trucked meat carcases around the eastern states. We could find no record that Wayne was employed by any of the businesses, so it was presumably related to the slaughtering or selling of cattle or meat.

Dave Schiller organised the next step, which was to conduct lightning inspections of all three businesses. As the inspectors arrived the companies were told that this was a widespread program to follow up on increased theft to livestock. To make it a bit more plausible his team also investigated three other businesses as well as the target ones.

The three non-target ones all turned out clean, as did one of the trucking companies. The meat processing plant had a number of cattle in a holding pen that had no ear tags or other identifying marks, and they were issued with an infringement notice. We'd decided not to come the heavy at the initial stage, so as to let the investigation continue without scaring people too much. The other trucking company was somewhat deficient in its paperwork, though we couldn't decide if it was deliberate fraud or simply office inefficiency. They were let off this time with a warning.

We did note when looking through the paperwork that one of the suppliers of cattle to the dodgy processing company had been a certain Wayne Robertson.

We discussed what we could do further, and Dave said: 'I don't think we're going to get very far with this sort of campaign. We may find a few more dodgy animals or carcases, but what's that really going to tell us? Unless we can find who the crooked large-scale suppliers to the meatworks are, we're not going to get the kingpins. We'll need to work out a better way to catch them in the act of duffing on graziers' properties, but that's much easier said than done.'

I said: 'How about a lot more random checks of stock transports of all sorts and sizes out around the grazing properties. They mightn't have had time to remove the ID marks if we get them straight after the act.'

Dave thought for a moment. 'For a murder squad man, that's not a bad idea. I'll draw up some plans and get some teams together.'

GIL REYNOLDS

I'd put the several large, bright orange blowflies that I'd collected with Millie in the forest north of here in a cage with decaying meat, and I'd noted at the time that at least one was laying eggs in the meat. I decided to leave them undisturbed for five to six days, by which stage the eggs should have hatched and the larvae developed to the third and final stage. That would be the best stage for identification.

A check at day five showed that they were still only second stage – it must have been a bit cooler in the shed than I'd realised, or else they had a slightly longer life cycle than typical flies, which can happen. I left them another three days and then took more samples, and I got some magnificent, large and well-developed larvae.

I took them back to the hotel, killed them and processed them for microscopic mounting. When I was able to examine the slide-mounts under the microscope, I got a result that I realised was going to make Alan Campbell's day. I was pretty excited myself – the larvae were identical to those that had been collected from Anna Ioannides' body. What I would need to do now is collect in forests for a way south of here to see if that particular fly occurred there, though it had never been seen south of here in previous collecting. If it didn't occur south of where Millie and I had caught it, that would show without much doubt that Anna's body must have lain around here, or even further north, for a while. A bit more evidence towards Wayne Robertson's guilt.

I called Alan and told him, and he was as pleased as I'd expected. He said it was a pity Australia didn't give knighthoods any longer or he'd have recommended me for one.

I just managed to catch Elsie before she left the hotel, and I asked her to tell Millie that the big orange fly had produced a very exciting result, and I'd tell her more about it when I next saw her.

Next day I began a detailed study of both the adult fly and the larvae, and by the end I was sure that it was a species new to science. In fact not just a new species but almost certainly a new genus. It definitely belonged to the family Calliphoridae, which were the blowflies, but it didn't fit very well into any of the known genera. I'd need to do a bit more work in a museum with a good collection of calliphorids before I could decide finally.

I began to speculate on an appropriate name in the circumstances. It wasn't vastly different from some of the *Calliphora* species, and one thing scientists often do in such a situation is to add a prefix to the name *Calliphora*. Something like *Pericalliphora* or *Paracalliphora* or similar. In this case I thought that a possibility would be *Annacalliphora*, as a tribute to poor Anna who after all first brought the species to scientific notice.

I couldn't say anything about the circumstances, of course, but something like "genus named for Anna Ioannides, who first brought it to scientific attention" should be all right.

Then there was the question of a species name, and I wondered if *milliae* might be appropriate, meaning "belonging to Millie". It was after all Millie who led me to the spot and drew my attention to it, thereby solving the whole problem. I could say "is named after young Kaantju woman Millie, who first collected the species near Coen in far north Queensland."

Annacalliphora milliae – it has a good ring to it. I like it.

ALAN CAMPBELL

Another Wednesday came along, and I think we were all beginning to think we were barking up the wrong tree. What if Elsie's mob had the wrong airstrip? What is it wasn't Wednesdays but some other day? What if they'd got wind of our investigation and switched to somewhere else?

However, a shout from Viktor at his screen put an end to that.

'Guys, the bleeper just went off, and I could see an aircraft landing at our strip. It came in from the east and taxied towards the trees where our gadget is, then turned and taxied back towards the other end. It's been met by a small wagon, and they seem to be transferring some boxes from one to the other. Here, have a look.'

As he said, there were various boxes being moved. Two people were doing the job – one at the aircraft unloading and one carrying to the truck and stacking them inside. Whether both men had come in the truck or one was the pilot of the aircraft Viktor couldn't say. The picture wasn't too bad, just slightly blurry.

'I got a good look at the aircraft as it turned close to the camera, and I've written down the letters and numbers on its tail – here.'

'Good, we can chase those up when it's gone.'

The box transfer appeared to have finished, and one of the men was handing a small package to the other man. Papers? Money? We couldn't judge. The one man then climbed into the aircraft, so he was presumably the pilot. The aircraft turned on its spot and took off towards the camera, soaring into the sky about three quarters of the way down the airstrip. The wagon swung round and drove off.

'Bugger,' said Viktor. 'I never got a good look at the rego of the wagon – the plane obscured it most of the time. I've got it all on tape, though. I can try a bit of image enhancement, though I'm not optimistic.'

From the approach of the aircraft it looked as though it had probably come in quietly from the east, over the Coral Sea. There would have been little or no aircraft surveillance in that area to pick it up as it flew in. The rego of the aircraft indicated that it was registered in Papua New Guinea, which wasn't at all surprising. We'd ask the authorities there if they could tell us more about it.

Ten minutes later Viktor came back to say that he might have a small bit of information on the vehicle's rego.

'I think the last two digits could have been a '9' and a '0', in one combination or another. Meaning 99, 00, 90 or 09 – they look rather the same when they're blurred. The first letter might have been an 'A' or an 'H'. Bit hard to tell.

'However, there's one other thing. If you look at this shot of the vehicle turning you can see that it's got a massive bull-bar thing on the front – one of those that comes up and is then bent a bit forwards at the top, and very strong construction. There aren't huge numbers of wagons with that sort of bull-bar, and combine it with the general look of the wagon, the black colour and the possible rego numbers, you might just be lucky and get somewhere.'

'Thanks, Viktor. We'll see what we can come up with.'

Merv said: 'Do you know if there are any CCTV cameras anywhere around there, or a reasonable way to the south? The vehicle's quite distinctive, and if we could get a clear rego that'd help a lot.'

I thought for a minute. 'I can get Gil to see if there are any in Coen. The petrol station there might have one for security, though I wouldn't bet on it. Then going south I'd be a bit surprised if there's one at Laura, but there could be one at the Mount Carbine petrol station. The vehicle would almost certainly have gone down that way – there isn't really anywhere else useful to go. But after Mount Carbine it could go to either Mareeba or Cairns, and then off in various directions.'

We agreed to follow all of these thoughts up and then re-convene.

* * *

You have to get lucky sometimes. We got nowhere checking truck regos – the possible digits that Viktor had picked up were too vague. However, the Mount Carbine petrol station did have CCTV, and a truck very like that from Viktor's video did stop there. The driver didn't get any petrol, but he went into the shop and the vehicle was parked where it could be clearly seen. None of us recognised the driver, but the rego was clearly readable, and we checked the ownership. It was registered to Malcolm Robertson Enterprises Proprietary Limited, which had a small fleet of vehicles in its name. Merv immediately said that we should get a tracker on that one too, and he would organise it.

* * *

One other line of investigation was also beginning to yield results. One of the places that one of Ioannides's trucks regularly went to after picking up meat was an address in Cairns – a moderate-sized and rather nondescript warehouse in Knight Street. A sign at the front said "Northern Logistics" – nothing else.

Merv decided that they should take a closer look, and he used a ploy that they'd apparently used before. He had one of his guys put on a boiler suit with Napier Rodent Control prominently on its top pocket, and he sent the guy together with a drug detector dog to the premises. The guy knocked at the door and said he was investigating reports of excessive numbers of rats in the area and could he just check their premises for anything that could be breeding rats inside? He told them the dog was trained to smell out rats. It was actually one of the drug detector dogs that was trained just to sit down if it sensed drugs, and it promptly sat down when it got inside.

'Bloody lazy thing,' said Merv's guy. He poked around the premises for a bit to make the rat thing seem genuine, then said: 'I can see your place is really neat and clean, and the lazy dog probably could too. There won't be any rats coming out of here, so we'll leave you in peace. Thank you for your time.'

To be on the safe side they did the same at several other premises in the area, in case anyone cross-checked. The dog didn't sit down in any of the other warehouses. We just had to hope that the people in the target premises weren't familiar with "passive" drug dogs, but they would be more likely to have known the ones that went berserk when they picked up drugs.

Merv had told the dog handler to note if there were any semi-trailer fuel tanks visible inside the premises that he and the dog entered, but he said he couldn't see any. However, he did say that there were various closed doors at the back, and there could have been anything behind those.

We followed up on all premises registered to Mal Robertson Enterprises, and kept a record in case any became of interest in the future. We were also hoping to identify the person who'd taken the drugs off the plane at the airstrip – we didn't have a name yet.

* * *

Another Wednesday came – only a week after the previous shipment at the airstrip, and this time another plane did come in. Same modus operandi, and same vehicle and person collecting the packages off the plane.

And this time we had a plan worked out. We reckoned that the vehicle would drive down to Cairns to offload at Robertson's warehouse, so we used the same strategy as with the Ioannides truck on the Bruce Highway. Just north of Mount Carbine we set up a truck inspection point – again it just looked like a random one, but we had a spotter car a bit north who could tell us when the target was approaching and we'd swing the operation into full gear.

The truck stopped, as it had to, and we told the driver that we were inspecting all vehicles to check for illegally transported wildlife. We didn't want any suspicion that it was a drug operation. We required him to open the back of the vehicle, and when we saw the boxes we made him open those as well.

'Well, mate, this doesn't look like illegal wildlife, but a whole lotta plastic packages filled with white powder looks remarkably like something else illegal. We're taking charge of this vehicle, and you're under arrest pending further investigation.'

The vehicle was driven to Cairns by a police driver, and Robertson's offsider was escorted in a separate police car. The driver was identified as Emilio Carbone, and subsequent analysis of the white powder showed that it was crystal meth. Further investigation of the packages revealed that others contained cocaine.

Under intensive questioning Carbone maintained that he was running a freelance operation. He got the drugs off someone he met in Coen – he didn't know the guy's name – and he was driving to Townsville to try to sell them. It was a very thin story, and highly implausible in the light of the quantity of drugs, but we didn't want to press too hard yet. He also didn't know that he'd been seen unloading the packages from a plane from PNG.

We agreed to hold Carbone for the moment, pending charges while we decided exactly how to go further with this without revealing our hand more fully.

GIL REYNOLDS

I was in my room at the hotel labelling some pinned flies when Elsie came in to clean the room.

"Morning, Gil. Okay if I do you now?'

'Fine, thanks, Elsie. How are you?'

'I'm good, thanks, but before I forget it I've got a message for you from your new assistant. She'd like to meet you once more at a weekend, and she reckons she can find some new and different flies for you.'

'Sounds interesting. I'll certainly be on for that one. I guess I should just front up with my collecting equipment and she'll do the rest?'

'Sort of, but she does want you to bring something else. She said to tell you to bring a small bucketful of fresh cow dung. Not too dry – sort of sloppy. She said you'll think that isn't important for blowflies, but you might just see.'

'This is getting even better.'

'And she'll bring something else herself, but I'm not to tell you. That'll be her surprise.'

'This is sounding really good now, but I'm not sure where

I could get fresh soft cow dung. I've seen some very dry stuff in the paddocks round here, but even when it comes out of the cows in this type of country it's pretty dry.'

'Well, I reckon you should go to the Coen shop and ask them. They've got a few dairy cows out the back for fresh milk to sell in the shop, and dairy cows put out nice soft stuff. They usually sell it to gardeners, but they wouldn't mind you getting a bucket for free if you tell 'em Elsie sent you.'

'D'you think next weekend should be okay for Millie? It's fine by me.'

'Don't reckon she'll be doing anything else. I'll tell her tonight.'

* * *

I got some nice soft cow dung from the Coen shop on the Friday, and Elsie took me to Millie early on the Saturday. Millie was dressed in good bush gear, and she had a couple of large packages with her. It didn't take too long to realise that they were fish. Distinctly old fish....

'Hi, Gil. You must be wondering what this is all about. You can probably smell the fish. They're because I've seen dead fish in the forest sometimes when someone's been catching them and they've dumped one or two, and I reckon the flies I've seen coming to them are a bit different from the ones on your dead meat. Some may be the same, but not all of them, so I thought we could see.

'And the cow dung that you've got – I've seen fresh droppings from wild pigs, and also from cassowaries, and a whole lot of flies come to them too. Most aren't like your sort, but I reckon a few are, and I thought you might like to see what does come along. I've read that some blowflies do come to droppings just to feed on them, so you never know.'

'Millie, this is great. But I'm intrigued at where you read that about the blowflies?'

'It was in one of the booklets that you brought me the other day. There was one on all sorts of insects, and in the bit on flies it said that.'

'Well, I'm really glad those pamphlets were some use. Now that you mention it I think I've read that blowflies do come and feed on fresh dung, even though they don't breed in it. The dung's full of bacteria, and that makes it good tucker for the flies, for developing their eggs. Anyway, let's go.'

We set out along another jungle track – I don't think it was the same one as last time. Thank God Millie appeared to know her way around here – I'd have been bushed straight away. We reached a small patch where the vegetation was less dense, and Millie said to put out some of the fish there and see what happens.

'I've only got these fish heads and tails. My cousin gave them to me. He kept the fish to eat, but I reckon these should do okay.'

Judging by the speed with which some flies arrived, they were more than okay. I got my net ready and watched to see what came. Some were definitely the same as those I'd been getting on rotten meat, but there were a few that did seem different and I netted a few of them.

We'd been standing in silence for some moments when Millie touched me gently and pointed to a tree just ahead of us.

'Carpet snake,' she murmured.

We stood and watched as a huge python wound its way along a tree branch, delicately reached across to the next tree and slid on to its nearest branch. It was dark brown with the most stunning paler brown and buff patterning all over its body, and the movements were unbelievably graceful. I've had carpet snakes in my roof in Brisbane, and they're generally welcome because they keep rats down, but it was another thing again seeing them in their native habitat like this.

Eventually it had slid out of sight, and we looked back at the fish bait. And what should there be but a fly, not a species that I knew, laying eggs into the operculum of one of the fish heads. We waited until it had finished and flown off, then I asked Millie if I could take the head back to the shed so that I could collect samples of the larval stages.

'That's what we're here for,' she whispered.

We decided to set the dung bait out in a different spot, and we moved on. Not along where the carpet snake had disappeared to, thank God.

Millie stopped again and said she thought this spot would be good, so I put out some of my bait. It was nice and smelly by that stage, and flies came to it pretty quickly. Most looked to my not very expert eye like species of the family Muscidae, which includes bushflies, house flies and some biting flies. Those sorts of flies are common all round Australia, and I think many of them do breed in dung.

One or two blowflies did also come to feed on the wet dung surface – all ones that I knew and had already collected. However, then there was a stunning arrival. It was a very large fly, looking like a blowfly but almost double the size of even a common bluebottle, which is a fair-sized fly in its own right. It was metallic green with a slight pattern of spots on the body, and lots of long and striking spines all over the abdomen. But perhaps the most striking feature was the head – large, red-brown eyes on either side, with quite vivid yellow between the eyes and all around them.

'This is the one I was hoping to find for you, Gil. This is the one I've seen before on cassowary droppings.'

'Millie, thank you so much for this. I've seen this in museum collections before, but I've never seen one in real life. And it's so much brighter and better when you see it alive. I'm trying to dredge back in my mind to what's known about it. It belongs to the blowfly family but it doesn't breed in dead meat or anything like that. I have a feeling that it's thought to be a parasite of snails, so I guess it's just come here for a feed.'

By that stage the fly had flown off again, and no more of that sort came back so I didn't have to decide whether to catch it for a collection or let such a beautiful creature continue to live. I think I would have left it anyway – they're already represented in museum collections.

In the same spirit of humanity I didn't take any others that came to the dung either, except for one small one that might be an unusual blowfly and I was keen to check out what it was. Then we called it a day, picked up the fish head sample and went back to meet Elsie. She had to put up with me having a stinking fish head all the way back to Pascoe Downs, but she didn't seem to mind. I think she was keen for me to encourage Millie's studies….

ALAN CAMPBELL

Merv sat with his small team, Dave Schiller and me to plan out the next stage of the investigation. He outlined where he thought we were at.

'I'm still trying to come to grips fully with who's doing what in this case, or more specifically these cases. We've actually got three areas of crime that we've all become involved in – the drugs importation from overseas, the cattle duffing and the murder of Anna Ioannides.

'With Anna's murder it seems increasingly clear that it was Wayne Robertson, probably acting alone. Maybe he was simply antagonised by Anna refusing him sex or something, or maybe she'd threatened to expose the illegal cattle trade that he also seems to be involved with. That's also plausible because Anna might have been trying to get back at her father. I reckon he's in all this up to his neck.

'Is Wayne also involved with the drugs side? I don't know but it seems quite possible. He could have been one of the people who collected shipments from the PNG plane before he had his prang, and he's a regular at Screwball in Townsville which we know is a hotspot for drug redistribution in Townsville.

'The person I'm having more trouble coming to grips with is Mal Robertson. I'm willing to bet that he's a kingpin in both the drugs and the illegal meat operations, but we haven't got any direct evidence against him at all yet.

'And finally there's Nicos Ioannides. I'm sure he's a kingpin in the illegal meat side, but he keeps himself at sufficient distance that there's no direct evidence yet that we can use. Is he also involved with the drugs side? No idea. It wouldn't surprise me, but again no evidence.

'So what are we going to do next? I'm still reluctant to show our hand too much. We've got the advantage that they don't know that we know about the drug planes, and where the trucks with trackers have gone. I think what I would favour is one targeted raid on just one of Mal Robertson Enterprise's premises, to see what we can find there. And what I'm thinking of is particularly records in offices rather than just drugs or something around the premises. It'll probably start warning them that something's up, but they won't know yet where we're coming from. Any thoughts on all that?'

Dave Schiller said: 'Seems sensible to me. I'd welcome any information you can dig out on the illegal meat trade, and you certainly wouldn't be stuffing up my wider investigation of who's doing what and where around the state.'

And my thoughts were pretty much the same. 'I don't imagine you'll be finding anything relating to Anna's murder. Unless her clothing turns up in one of the filing drawers, of course. We've never found her gear, but I don't think it's very likely to be in an office either. But what you're proposing certainly won't do my case any harm.'

'Thanks, guys. As I said, we'll probably alert them a bit, but it might be interesting just what we then prod them into doing. They might give things away a bit further.'

GIL REYNOLDS

Millie's fish head was really paying off. I managed to get first, second and third stage larvae plus pupae from it, and I was then able to pin a few adult flies once I'd hardened them off. The female must have laid a lot of eggs in it while we were watching. Some species have large batches, others much fewer. And even better, it did turn out to be a species that I'd never found in meat. It wasn't one I knew at all, though it might be in museum collections somewhere.

I was getting some really interesting results from this whole study in the northern Cape York Peninsula, to the point where I could probably be able to publish an overall report of findings in a scientific journal. And if that happened it would only be fair to include my new assistant as co-author.

Sadly this probably also represented the closing stage of what has been a very nice sojourn in the north. I was made most welcome by all the folk up here – Stuey, Ray Smith, Chaz and others, and most of all Elsie and Millie. Elsie was an amazing woman in her quiet way. No fuss, but she knew exactly what she wanted to do and where she intended to go, and she just did it.

I had both admiration and affection for Elsie, and one of the things she was determined to do was get a future for Millie. She obviously realised as much as I now did what future potential Millie had, and I'd have to give more thought on how I could go on helping her. Something to discuss with Nicole when I get back to Brisbane.

ALAN CAMPBELL

We decided to wait until the next delivery of drugs came to the airstrip before we took any further action. On the next Wednesday but one a shipment arrived. We watched the unloading via the hidden camera – it was the same wagon with the very large bull-bar that picked the boxes up. We picked it up as it reached the outskirts of Cairns, and it went to the Robertson Enterprises depot in Knight Street. As soon as it was inside our task force followed it in, and we raided the place.

As well as today's drug shipment we found some containers of drugs that must have been from a previous shipment, stashed in cupboards around the place. Three of our force started interrogating the four men who were in the premises at the time, while two of us went into the office and began searching through all the papers and files that we could find.

No cash was found in the premises – that was presumably held somewhere else. However, the main office computer showed very large amounts of money having been received by a particular account, in the name of M. Robertson Enterprises.

Even on a first quick reading the files were very revealing

– correspondence and emails between Mal Robertson and something called Bird of Paradise Holdings in Port Moresby, covering numerous drug shipments into Australia. Even better, there were invoices for onward shipments of the drugs from Cairns to Ioannides Proprietary Limited at a depot in Melbourne – not the address of his large meatworks, but separate premises in Collingwood.

The whole trove was going to need a lot of analysis. We didn't want to maximise alarm by taking everything away, so instead we'd brought a small scanner and a computer with us, and we went through copying everything that seemed of interest on to the computer. Then the files and records were put back much as they'd been before we came, and the task of careful analysis began back in police headquarters.

* * *

A bit later on Merv brought us together again and said: 'We've finally had some information from PNG about the plane that's been coming in to our airstrip. It's registered to a company called Bird of Paradise Air Charter. It's usually chartered just for a day or so, and on the days in question it was hired by something called United Freight. We can't find anything out about United Freight – it seems to be just a convenient name. The PNG guys got the impression that Bird of Paradise wasn't too worried about who was getting the plane as long as it was paid for. They had no idea who United Freight were, and the PNG authorities didn't know anything either. The authorities have told Bird of Paradise to let them know the next time United charters a plane so that they can check up on who United really is.

'The other news is that we've also been doing some surveillance inside Ioannides Meats. We've had an undercover person in the main office of Ioannides Meats for some weeks now. She's in the accounts office, and she's been watching for anything suspicious but also anything that might suddenly be changing. If Mal's been in touch with old man Ioannides as a result of our raid, they may be taking some steps to cover things up a bit, and I'd like to get a handle on that. We've squared it with the Vics that we can do surveillance on their territory without getting noses out of joint.'

MARION

Our time at Flyblown Downs would be coming to an end soon. The grant that I'd been given was just about finished, and so too was the work. I felt I'd managed to conclude a good study, and I would be surprised if the government conservation body that gave me the grant wasn't also happy with it.

Nicholas too had achieved more than he'd expected when he started, and we'd both be going away with happy memories of some of the Australian characters we'd encountered on the trip, and vivid memories of some of the fabulous outback landscapes. When we first arrived I think we both thought that the scenery looked rather dry and dull, but since then we'd certainly learned to appreciate and love it.

We told Frank and Mike that we'd be moving on soon, and they seemed quite regretful. I guess it was going to be somewhat lonely with just the two of them there. Mike said he was particularly disappointed because Frank didn't appreciate his cooking, and his two best customers would be disappearing. We'd certainly enjoyed his inventiveness, not to mention his bubbly personality.

Frank told us that Mike and Lorraine, the jillaroo at Miranda Downs, were thinking of setting up a luxury camping resort in the area once Mike's present contract had finished. They were thinking somewhere near Normanton on the coast of the Gulf Country, with Mike doing the catering side and Lorraine doing more of the technical work and organising.

Frank said: 'Lorraine'll be good at the practical work. Tandouris wouldn't know the difference between a distributor cap and a hub cap, but Lorraine can fix absolutely anything. But on the flip side, her idea of cooking a steak is to put it on the barbie for half an hour on the one side, then turn it over for another half hour. Then ten minutes more on the first side to make sure it's done. Then you use it to re-sole your boot because it's no good for eating. But as you've seen, Mike does a mean camp meal.'

I thought that was good news. They were a nice pair, and they should be able to make a good go of something like that.

Nicholas suggested that we should contact Gil to tell him that we were going to up sticks, and we got him on Frank's phone.

'Gil, it's Marion here. I'm just ringing to let you know that we've basically finished our projects here. We'll probably be off back to Brisbane in a few days' time. It's all gone pretty well, and we'd like to thank you in particular for making it all so easy and productive for us.'

'Well, I knew this moment would come sometime, but I'll be sorry to see you go. You fitted pretty well into our bizarre set-up – even managed to put up with Tandouris's cooking.'

'That wasn't a hardship. Believe me, we had a lot worse

in some of the places we worked in Africa. This was five-star dining!'

'Look, I've just had a thought. Are you in a great hurry to get back to Brisbane? If not, why don't you come up this way for a few days? You've seen the arid part of north Queensland – now come and see some of the fabulous rainforest. We might even be able to find you a cassowary in the wild, and if we're really lucky a bird of paradise or a tree kangaroo. The birds aren't as amazing as the PNG ones, but they're still not bad. I know Nicholas did have the one trip up here, but he was a bit crook at the time, and we were after crims rather than wildlife then. What do you reckon?'

'Hang on and I'll just check with Nicholas.' A quick consultation with Nicholas, and then I said: 'Nicholas says just try and hold him back!'

'Great. I can organise one or two things before you come. My own study's winding up too now – it's gone pretty well, partly thanks to my new assistant who you can meet when you get here.' There seemed to be a bit of a chuckle in his voice as he said that. 'So when do you think you might be here?'

'It'll take us a bit of time to finalise everything here. Maybe about three weeks or so from now. Where exactly would we find you when we do come?'

'I'm in Coen, which is a reasonable-sized settlement, and there's a pub here. I can organise you a room there – it's not the height of the season at the moment.'

'Great, you're on. We'll give you another call a bit before we leave here, so you'll know roughly when we'll be with you.'

ALAN CAMPBELL

Naomi, Merv's plant in the accounts office of Ioannides Meats, was reporting some unusual activity in several offices. There was some large-scale removal of files, and Nicos Ioannides, who was normally hardly ever seen outside his inner sanctum, was suddenly in and out of his office a lot. He was also huddled with several senior staff at times, and he generally looked rather grim. Not that he was ever seen with much of a smile.

We discussed this and decided to let things stew for a bit longer, and we got back to Naomi to ask her to keep a further close eye on things and keep us posted.

* * *

Meanwhile, the team that was examining the paperwork and computer material from the Knight Street depot was coming up with some really good results. United Freight in Papua New Guinea turned out to be owned by something called Australasian Holdings, which in turn belonged to Mal Robertson Enterprises. United Freight had links to a Chinese company, which was no doubt the supplier of the drugs that were coming in, but we couldn't tell anything from their Chinese name. We would be trying to get more information from the Chinese authorities, which might or might not be forthcoming.

There were also detailed financial records, which was pretty careless of Mal Robertson to have them so readily available. They gave us not only the money trail but also the names of individuals and companies that were involved. A number of people would be getting visits from Merv and his team in the coming days.

There wasn't anything, however, about dodgy meat transactions, and our guess was that that material might be inside one of the other warehouses owned by Mal's company. We agreed that we'd exposed our hand so much by now that there wasn't any point in trying to keep anything else secret, so we decided to raid both the Spoto Street and Gatton Street warehouses in Cairns.

Spoto Street turned out to be the one. It was a cold storage depot, mostly full of butchered beef carcases. There weren't many paper records there, but their computer had wide-ranging information and records. Interestingly, they implicated quite a few more people than Dave Schiller had picked up before. They also revealed the large extent to which Wayne Robertson had been involved in the dodgy meat business. And furthermore, a large proportion of the shipments had gone to Ioannides' Meats in Melbourne. What a surprise that was....

A quick further consultation between Merv, myself and

Dave agreed that Dave would now concentrate fully on the meat side, and Merv and I would take the drugs side further. The one figure that straddled two investigations was Wayne Robertson, in relation to both meat and Anna's murder. We agreed that Wayne should be arrested on the meat charges at this stage, and we'd hold the murder evidence in abeyance for a bit longer. We were still of the belief that he didn't know what we'd found out from the back of his wagon.

On the drugs side we agreed that Merv and I should go to Mount Spec, to interview Mal Robertson with a view to arresting him on drugs charges. We hadn't put any direct surveillance on the property, but we were monitoring traffic in both directions along the Mount Spec road and he hadn't come down there to the coast highway.

* * *

We duly travelled to the Mount Spec property. As we approached it we saw the same fine old Queenslander with the wide timber verandahs that we remembered. Worryingly, though, it looked somewhat closed up. We drove up to the front steps, went up to the front door and knocked. After a moment the door was opened by Mal Robertson.

'Mr Robertson, I'm Inspector Merv Tansley of the Australian Federal Police. We're investigating the importation of drugs into Australia from Papua New Guinea, and we have reason to believe that some of your properties in north Queensland have been involved in the importations."

'I think there's been some mistake there. I deal in meat and some other commodities, but certainly not drugs. If you've got evidence of any such involvement it must be by some of my employees, not by me.'

The bastard was going to try and sacrifice some of his staff to save himself. He had Buckley's of doing that.

'Look, come inside and we can discuss this further. You can show me what evidence you've got and I'll answer it.'

We went inside and into the same front room in which Mrs Robertson had put us when we visited that first time.

We sat down and Mal said: 'I'll just get a copy of my staff registers so we can see who does what in which premises', and he walked out.

A second later Merv gave me a look of alarm and we raced to the door, but we were just too late. We heard a key turning and found the door locked. We each went over to a window and tried to open it, but the windows were locked as well.

'Bugger, bugger, bugger' said Merv. 'The bastard obviously knew we were coming, and he set this up to trap us. I'll call Jake who's at the bottom of the Mount Spec road and tell him to detain Mal as soon as he drives down there.'

We tried the door and the windows again, but none of them wanted to open. We tried shoulder-charging the door, but the frame must have been made of very hard old wood and it wouldn't give. Likewise the windows.

In the end we picked up one of the chairs in the room, and smashed our way out of one of the windows, though that took some work too. We climbed out through the wreckage and ran around the property, but Mal had gone. Even worse, he'd slashed the tyres of our wagon, so we had no way of getting back to the highway. We had to call Jake again and ask him to send someone up with another vehicle to rescue us.

Merv said: 'I'm never going to live this down when we get back to headquarters. It's personal now.'

The rescue car eventually arrived and we climbed in. We figured that at least Mal should have been detained further down the road, but when we got to Jake he said he hadn't seen hide nor hair of Mal.

'Christ,' said Merv, 'It just gets worse. I didn't think that there was any back way out of Mal's property, but there must have been.'

He called up a map of the area on his phone. It showed a track heading down to Mal's paddocks, but it appeared that it then went out further west towards public roads heading both west and south. It seemed very likely that that was the way that Mal went, and he'd be well away by now. All we could do then was put out a national alert for his arrest, and hope.

GIL REYNOLDS

In anticipation of Marion and Nicholas's visit I'd booked a room for them from Stuey, and I'd told Elsie about them and their backgrounds. I suggested that Millie might like to meet them, and if she didn't mind show them some of the birds of her country. Maybe even a tree kangaroo if that was possible. Elsie was very enthusiastic. I think she wanted to give Millie as much contact with other biologists as possible.

Marion and Nicholas arrived on a Thursday, after a pretty long trip. We gave them the Friday to recover and have a poke around locally. We'd lined up the visit to Millie on the Saturday, and I warned them to wear something that covered their legs. 'I know you went around in shorts in the bush at Flyblown, but if you do that in the forest here you'll be the target of every leech for miles around.'

Next morning we made an early start, and Millie was waiting for us when we got to the school. I gave out a bottle of water to each person, and Millie had brought some of the biscuits made from ground grass seeds that I'd tried before. She thought that the visitors might be interested to try them. We drove to the start of one of the forest tracks, and set off walking. Millie said: 'My cousin told me this might be the best area to see a tree kangaroo.'

I could see Marion and Nicholas staring in wonder at the lush and diverse tropical forest vegetation. At one point Millie showed them one of the bush fruits – I still hadn't picked up its name – and she invited us all to try one. They were delicious. Slightly acid, but with a beautiful fruity flavour.

A bit further along Millie held up a hand, and we then crept forward very quietly. Ahead was a cassowary and one chick, the chick about the same age as the two she'd shown me previously. And as with the earlier one that Millie and I had seen, the mother suddenly sensed us and was off.

We continued on the track, and Millie pointed out the lawyer vines that loved to grab clothing of passing people and were very hard to disentangle. She also pointed out a stinging tree and said: 'You get stung by one of those and you'll remember it for quite a while.'

We walked on for a bit, but didn't see anything very special, and after a bit Millie said: 'I think we should try another track that I know. We might see a bit more there.'

Back to the vehicle and a short drive, and then we were off along another track. Again we walked for a bit, and then Millie held up her hand. She put her hand to her ear, and we all listened. There was a loud bird call that was a sort of "whee-you, whee-you" repeated, ending with just a "whee".

'That's one of the special birds" whispered Millie. We all peered, and tried to home in on the sound but it was one of those shrill calls that reverberated and you couldn't pin down the location. However, finally Millie pointed to high up in a tree. 'I think that might be it, but it's hard to see that far away.

Marion pulled out a pair of binoculars from her backpack and peered at the bird, then she nodded. She handed the binoculars to Millie, and showed her how to focus them. When she twigged how to do it, the reaction was rather like when she looked down my microscope for the first time – wide-eyed amazement.

'Wow, that's fantastic. And that bird. I've never seen it like that before.'

Marion pulled out a copy of Slater's "Field Guide to Australian Birds" and looked up Birds of Paradise. After perusal of the distribution maps, the calls and the markings and colour of the bird, she said it must be a male Magnificent Rifle-bird. It was black on the back, iridescent green and purple on the top of the head and on the breast, and then an iridescent golden-green band separating that from a purplish black abdomen. A dramatic bird.

Then, even better, it went into what must have been its courtship display. It curved its two wings up, either side of the head, until they came up almost to touch each other. At the same time the head vanished, so that there was just a blackish crescent shape with the brilliant purple iridescence of the throat shining in the middle. We all looked in turn through the binoculars, and we were all speechless. It may not have been as exotic as the best of the PNG birds of paradise, but it was certainly the most amazing bird that I'd ever seen. Even Millie looked totally awed.

Anything else would have been an anticlimax, but we did see one other thing of note on the way back – an enormous python with a huge bulge in its middle. It was somewhat stretched out as I don't think it could have curled up with that bulge, and it was quiescent as it digested whatever it had eaten. Maybe that was as close as we were going to get to a tree kangaroo, because I'd read that they were one of the prey of large pythons. We certainly didn't see any live tree kangaroos on this trip.

When we got back to Millie's school, the teacher Julie just happened to be walking close by, so we took the chance to introduce Marion and Nicholas. When Marion said that they'd just come from the Gulf country Julie asked: 'Which part were you in?'

'We were in a bush camp not very far from a cattle station called Miranda Downs.'

Julie looked delighted. 'Oh, I know that well. My brother's a stockman at Miranda. I'm from the Gulf myself – near Normanton.'

Then there followed a detailed discussion of Julie's country, much of which Marion had managed to see. Millie just stood there looking rapt.

Before we left Millie asked if she could look at Marion's copy of Slater's Field Guide to Australian Birds. She leafed through page after page, totally fascinated.

'Wow, this is so good.' She looked at me. 'I wonder if Nicole in Brisbane could get me a copy of this? I'd be happy to pay her for it.'

Marion said: 'I've got a much better idea. I would like to give you this copy of the book. I'll be going back to the UK soon, and I can easily get another copy of it there. And there are actually two books – Parts One and Two. It would make me very happy if you'd accept them, please.'

Millie looked very embarrassed and didn't know what to say, so I said quickly: 'I think that's a great idea. Nicole mightn't be able to get it all that easily in Brisbane anyway.'

Marion then said: 'When I was a student I had a lot of help and encouragement from other people who were experts. I think they thought I had an interest in their birds and they just wanted to make me go on. Now I can see that you already know a lot about birds and animals and plants generally, and even more importantly I can see that you love them, so I'd like to give you one more gift.' And she held out the binoculars.

Millie gasped. 'Oh, I really couldn't accept this. You'll need it yourself.'

'Millie, again I can get a replacement easily in the UK, and you can't easily get any here. Please accept them. The only thing that I ask is that you go on studying and loving the birds. And one day you can write to me and tell me all the things you've learned about them.'

Millie was still quite embarrassed, so I said: 'I can't think of a better home for these binoculars. And just think, Marion, now you'll have more room in your baggage for souvenirs of Australia to take back to the Poms!'

Back in the hotel that evening, dining on Stuey's best dinner menu – steak, what else? – we toasted Millie with some of the quite reasonable Australian Riesling that Stuey had dug out of the hotel cellar. And I was really pleased that Marion and Nicholas had made the extra trip. It was obvious how much extra encouragement it had given Millie. Not to mention two bird books and some binoculars….

* * *

Next morning Marion and Nicholas were off to Brisbane and then the UK. We promised to keep in touch, and I said I'd let them know how the various crime cases turned out. Elsie also came and farewelled them – she'd heard of their gifts to Millie, and she was probably at least as appreciative as Millie of that.

And then sadly I had to start planning my departure too. It had begun to feel like home up here, but my fly and maggot study had done all it could up this way. My next job would be to sort out the identities and names of all the species and describe all the stages of the maggots. The National Museum of Victoria, which had the most relevant collection in Australia, had offered me a corner in one of their labs, and my boss had approved a travel allowance to enable me to live down there. Just…. It would probably be Old Mother Bailey's bed and breakfast or its equivalent, but it would do.

The farewells were warm and sad, but I promised to keep in touch, in particular over Millie's education.

ALAN CAMPBELL

Merv called us together for a quick consultation, and we agreed that we should now go for a confrontation at Ioannides Meats. He put together a fair-sized team to avoid any repetition of the earlier problems. Those of us in Brisbane flew to Melbourne and picked up transport, and we met with the local AFP personnel who had already been undertaking a lower-key investigation of Ioannides Meats.

There hadn't been any sightings of Mal Robertson and his wife yet, but we decided that it could be useful to take Wayne Robertson, who was now in custody, with us to confront Nicos Ioannides.

I thought I owed Gil Reynolds a call to update him on what was happening, given that his work up at Coen had partly put us where we are now. To my surprise I found that he'd also just arrived in Melbourne, and was working on his flies at the National Museum of Victoria. I suggested to Merv that it might be a plus to have Gil along as well when we went into the meat factory, and he seemed to think that was a good idea.

Naomi had previously secured a detailed plan of the Ioannides site and the various buildings for us, and we went straight into the meat processing hall which was the central part of the operation. The various offices, including Ioannides' suite, came off that, and anyone leaving any of the offices would have to come through that central hall.

On arrival we went to the reception desk and said that we needed to meet with Mr Ioannides. The receptionist looked doubtful and said she didn't think he was there at the moment. We showed her our police IDs and said this was an official investigation. She gulped and said she'd better call Mr Ioannides' personal secretary. The secretary arrived, looking at us as though we were some sort of unwelcome contamination in an otherwise pristine environment. The refrigeration units in the building weren't the only chilly things around – the secretary's look was pretty close.

Merv said: 'We'd like to meet with Mr Ioannides immediately, please. We're undertaking an important investigation into illegal movements of meat, and we believe he may have some involvement in these.'

A shadow of a smile passed over the secretary's face. 'I'm sorry but Mr Ioannides is not here at the moment.'

'So where would he be at this moment?'

'He's currently visiting his elderly mother, who is not well at present.'

'And where would his mother be?'

'She lives in Chora, which is the capital of the island of Patmos in the eastern Aegean Sea. Chora stands at the top of the mountain in the middle of the island. It's a most beautiful place.' Her smile as she said it was distinctly smug, though it must have been bittersweet because she would have known what was about to happen to the business in which she worked.

Merv said to me: 'The bastard! He's done a runner. The rats are all leaving their sinking ships, but the buggers are just a step ahead of us each time.'

Wayne Robertson was standing near Merv, and he was smirking even more than Nicos's secretary as Merv said that. He muttered loudly: 'Ha, bloody ha!'

However, one lot of rats hadn't quite left their sinking ship, because at that moment Mal Robertson stormed into the central meat hall, with his wife a bit of a way behind him. Mrs Robertson was looking as though she wished she was anywhere but in the meat hall. She was clutching her little dog Bandy to her, maybe for comfort as much as anything.

Mal probably wasn't expecting any of us to be there, and he didn't notice us at first. The first person his eyes lit on was his son Wayne. He went apoplectic red, and he yelled out: 'You stupid, cretinous bloody fuckwit – you've bloody well brought all this on us. If you hadn't killed that bloody girl none of this would have happened! We'd have been cruising along just like we always have.'

A look of horror came over Mrs Robertson's face, and she fainted. The little dog somehow avoided the falling body and dropped to the floor by itself, then ran off into the distance across the hall floor. Gil Reynolds ran after it.

A number of people rushed to the assistance of Mrs Robertson, and one person ran up with a stretcher and a de-fibrillator. An ambulance was called for, and the paramedics eventually revived Mrs Robertson, who was then taken away in the ambulance for further medical attention.

While this was going on Merv was watching Mal Robertson, who had now noticed us and seemed to be looking rather too keenly at ways to get out of the building again. There was no way Merv was going to let him get away once more. Robertson then demanded that he be allowed to accompany his wife in the ambulance, but Merv told him that he was under arrest for drug trafficking and illegal meat trading. A policewoman would accompany Mrs Robertson in the ambulance, and report back as appropriate.

After a quick confab about Wayne, we decided that Merv would also arrest him on drug charges rather than have me arresting Wayne for murder. The drug charges were federal and Merv had the relevant jurisdiction in Melbourne, but the murder was a Queensland offence and we'd have had to ask the Victoria Police to arrest him and then we'd have had to seek extradition. Better to get him for the drugs first, take him to Brisbane on that charge and then hit him with murder once he was back there. And Mal's outburst should be the last nail in Wayne's coffin for that one.

Mal and Wayne both had their mobile phones taken away, and both were taken away but in separate vehicles. We weren't having them cobbling together any dubious stories or plans this time.

* * *

The charges were laid, and the slow wheels of the judicial procedures began to run. We all spent the next few weeks assembling evidence to build the best possible and most comprehensive cases against Mal and Wayne Robertson, and against Nicos

Ioannides for the extradition application. We didn't expect this last to get much traction, at least not in the foreseeable future, but we had to go through with it.

Mrs Robertson eventually recovered from what had turned out to be a heart attack. She was a shadow of her former self, but that was probably due to the destruction of her family as much as anything else. She must have known at least broadly what was going on, but she'd no doubt have tried very hard not to see it. We hadn't found any evidence of direct involvement so she didn't face any charges. Her punishment was already sufficient in my view.

We did, however, round up a number of employees of Mal Robertson Enterprises, and charged them to whatever extent we were able to find relevant evidence in all the files and computers. Overall it was going to represent a significant reduction in drugs on Australian streets, which was a major plus.

The Papua New Guinea authorities went to follow up on Australasian Holdings and United Freight which had been involved in chartering the plane that flew to our airstrip, but both had mysteriously vanished. Their premises were empty when raided, and no drugs or records were found anywhere. You never win everything.

EPILOGUE: ALAN CAMPBELL

Three months after the showdown at the meatworks – if you could call it that – I met with Merv Tansley over a beer in Brisbane. We discussed whether or not we could consider the case an overall success.

We agreed that it had been a significant success against two unpleasant criminals, Wayne and Mal Robertson. Both were under arrest, with very strong cases against them for drug trafficking and for illegal meat trading and stock theft. Further, Wayne had been charged with the murder of Anna Ioannides. A number of their offsiders were also facing various degrees of prosecution, and the Screwball Disco in Townsville had been closed down. We'd decided not to prosecute Vic who'd worked there – she had after all given Nicholas some useful information relating to Anna's murder, and also about Wayne Robertson.

The one principal in both the drugs and the meat cases who'd escaped arrest was Nicos Ioannides. Merv said: 'When I heard that day that Ioannides had done a runner I was furious,

262

and I reckoned that because of that he'd escaped any punishment. But since then I've been thinking that maybe I was wrong about that. There's currently an arrest warrant out for him, which means that if he comes back into Australia he'll be arrested immediately. We've applied to the Greek authorities to have him extradited, but I'm not holding my breath over that one. Even under the best of conditions that'll probably take years, and he'll be able to hire the best lawyers in Greece who'll delay it even further, if not indefinitely.

'But just think what he's actually forfeited. His plant in Melbourne's been seized under proceeds of crime legislation. It's been put under some official receivers who are in the process of disposing of it, and he won't get any of the resulting funds. So he's lost his assets, and a factory that was probably his pride, and he's lost one of his daughters. I think he is being punished in the end anyway.

'And it's his fault that he got caught in the first place. If he hadn't been greedy and shipped human bodies inside a meat truck, we would never have impounded the truck, and if we hadn't impounded it we wouldn't have found the drugs in the fake fuel tank, and he'd still be importing and dealing them.'

I grinned at Merv, and said: 'Hi ho, Silver. And the Lone Ranger rides off into the sunset. Pretty well done, mate....'

AND BACK IN TIME, A TAILPIECE....

In the kerfuffle surrounding Mal Robertson's arrest at the meatworks, Mrs Robertson had fallen to the floor in a dead faint. It didn't appear to be any sort of diversionary ploy – she was definitely out cold.

She'd been holding her dog, little Bandy, who also fell to the floor but was unharmed, and we saw him scamper off. Gil Reynolds chased him, and both disappeared from view.

When Gil reappeared somewhat later, he was alone.

Alan Campbell looked pointedly at Gil.

'What happened to the dog?'

'Dog?' said Gil, with extreme vagueness. 'What dog would that be?'

'That bloody overgrown rat that belonged to the Robertsons. Little Bandy or whatever it was called.'

'Oh, that dog,' said Gil, as though no dog had been further from his mind. 'Little Bandicoot Fuckwit.' He paused for a moment, then said: 'It was a terrible tragedy, actually. I chased it along the factory floor, but it suddenly veered off and ran up the steps that went up to the inspection catwalk above the mincing tanks.

'It ran along the walkway, but it's a very narrow catwalk and it has a shiny and slippery surface. I suppose that's to make it easier to clean. Anyway, the dog was floundering all over the surface and slipping. I tried to grab it, but it slid sideways and into one of the machines. According to the sign on the tank it's now one of the ingredients of Bavarian mettwurst, destined for the greater Sydney area.'

He paused and tried to look grieving, but it wasn't working. 'The tragedy was that I was trying to head it towards the machine that was making frankfurts. I really would have liked to think of it being marketed across the nation as the ultimate in Hot Dogs….'

AUTHOR'S NOTE

All characters in this book are fictional, and none relates to an actual person. Their general characteristics are based on people I met while working in the Gulf Country and Cape York Peninsula, but only in the broadest way.

There are many different blowflies in Papua New Guinea, with many still waiting to be discovered. However, *Calliphora aiyurensis* is not one of them. It can cause taxonomic problems if genuine species are cited out of context, so I deliberately made up a fictitious name.

However, the point made in the story that there are many close parallels between the faunas of Papua New Guinea and far northern Australia is entirely correct. Tree kangaroos and birds of paradise are mentioned in the story, and there are many others among animals and plants too. The blowflies of far northern Australia are still not well known (I was able to collect new species with some quite casual collecting when I worked there), and there will undoubtedly be many parallels like the one in this book.

The details of characteristics of maggots by which they are identified are entirely accurate, and I thank a number of people for having encouraged my studies in that area – in particular my good friend Adrian Pont of the British Museum (Natural History) for having started me off and encouraged me over many years, Doug Waterhouse for having found a grant that got me going, and Don Colless of the Australian National Insect Collection, who knew far more about flies than I ever did.

I am also very grateful to several people who have encouraged and advised my attempts at writing – in particular Vashti Farrer, Barbara Walsh and Maureen Cashman.

Finally, I thank my wife Pam for having put up with the maggots for many years – far beyond any call of duty...

ABOUT THE AUTHOR

Paul Ferrar is a biologist who worked on dung beetles and maggots in northern Australia, on termites in a South African game park, as a rat-catcher in a large mental hospital in the UK, and in the Australian aid program managing cooperative research projects between Australian agricultural scientists and those in developing countries working on similar problems.

He is also the author of a 907-page monograph on all you ever wanted to know and more about the maggots of 96 different families of flies.

He is married to a very tolerant wife, also a research scientist and administrator but fortunately with a more conventional career.